This Is It

"I wasn't kidding when I said I haven't done this since I was seven or eight," Eric said, pulling his skatelace tight with one hand and hanging on to the door of his cream-colored Mustang with the other. "I guess this is it," he said, pushing himself off from the car and across the paved lot. Instantly his legs shot out from under him.

"Watch it!" Katie cried, impulsively grabbing his hand before he could go down completely. His fingers closed tightly around hers. "Don't worry. I won't let you fall," she said.

COUPLES

Books from Scholastic
in the **Couples** series:

#1 *Change of Hearts*
#2 *Fire and Ice*
#3 *Alone, Together*
#4 *Made for Each Other*
#5 *Moving Too Fast*
#6 *Crazy Love*
#7 *Sworn Enemies*
#8 *Making Promises*
#9 *Broken Hearts*
#10 *Secrets*
#11 *More Than Friends*
#12 *Bad Love*
#13 *Changing Partners*
#14 *Picture Perfect*
#15 *Coming on Strong*
#16 *Sweethearts*
#17 *Dance with Me*
#18 *Kiss and Run*
#19 *Show Some Emotion*
#20 *No Contest*

Couples Special Editions
Summer Heat!
Be Mine!

Coming Soon . . .
#21 *Slow Dancing*

NO CONTEST

by M.E. Cooper

SCHOLASTIC INC.
New York Toronto London Auckland Sydney

Scholastic Books are available at special discounts for quantity purchases for use as premiums, promotional items, retail sales through specialty market outlets, etc. For details contact: Special Sales Manager, Scholastic Inc., 730 Broadway, New York, NY 10003.

No part of this publication may be reproduced in whole or in part, or stored in a retrieval system, or transmitted in any form or by any means, electronic, mechanical, photocopying, recording, or otherwise, without written permission of the publisher. For information regarding permission, write to Scholastic Inc., 730 Broadway, New York, NY 10003.

ISBN 0-590-40425-3

Copyright © 1987 by Cloverdale Press. Cover photo: Pat Hill, copyright © 1987 by Cloverdale Press. All rights reserved. Published by Scholastic Inc.

12 11 10 9 8 7 6 5 4 3 2 1   7 8 9/8 0 1 2/9

Printed in the U.S.A.   01

First Scholastic printing, March 1987

Chapter 1

Varsity gymnast Katie Crawford sat on the windowsill of the student activities room at Kennedy High, wishing with all her heart that Chris Austin's top secret emergency meeting of representatives from all the school's athletic teams was over. Katie sighed and peered up from under her bangs to check the black metal clock hanging over the chalkboard. It was ten after three and the meeting hadn't even started yet. In fact, the usually punctual Chris hadn't even turned up. Chris's boyfriend, Greg Montgomery, founder of Kennedy's crew team, hadn't arrived, either. Maybe Kennedy's efficient student body president and her boyfriend had both come down with a sudden bout of spring fever. Katie knew it was going around; she had a mean case of the fever herself. The symptoms were unmistakable: a desire to be outdoors all the time, at all costs; a crazy urge to toss school books into the Potomac and go roller skating. For days, Katie had been feeling like she was about to burst.

Wishing she were out in the bright sunshine right now, Katie reached out the open window and stroked the soft, downy petal of a blossom just outside the window. Spring! Spring! Spring! She felt like screaming at the top of her lungs. She felt that good, that happy, and that alive.

Just last night, she had won her third gymnastics competition in a row and had nearly catapulted the Kennedy girls' gymnastics team into the state finals. Only a couple more meets were left before the states, and the team was just a few points short of securing a berth among the top competitors throughout Maryland. Katie was proud of her performance. All the extra hours at the school gym and with her own gymnastics teacher, Mr. Romanski, at the Georgetown Martial Arts, Fitness, and Dance Center, had paid off. She had worked hard to make this year her personal best, and so far it had been.

The loud crack of a bat against a ball resounded across the quad. Katie looked toward the baseball field. The boys' team was taking batting practice. Right fielder Tommy Derringer was up at the plate. She recognized him by his stance and the shock of blond curls poking out from under his baseball cap. Last year she'd had an A-Number-One crush on Tommy, but he had only been interested in her as a pal. At the start of baseball season he had walked her home every afternoon for a week, talking statistics, sizing up the current Orioles' lineup, and drawing the battle lines between the teams in the American League

East. But then she discovered he was more interested in getting to know her dad than her. Katie's father had once played left field in the Orioles' farm system and now was a top scout for the club.

Tommy had been the first real crush of her life, and Katie chalked it up as being a basic part of sophomore slump. Before last spring, she had always thought of guys as friends — people she hung out with or ran races against, or dared to match her uncanny ability to shimmy up a lamp post, climb to the top of the tallest tree, or walk on top of the tall fences along the backyards of the houses in the quiet neighborhood of Rose Hill where she lived. But after Tommy, everything had changed. Since then she had had three more legitimate crushes, and every time it was the same. None of the guys had seemed to notice she was a girl, even when she began using mascara on her long dark lashes, pierced her ears, and tied ribbons around her straight red ponytail. Now that it was spring of her junior year, she was beginning to get depressed about it. Practically everyone she knew was part of a couple, and here she was, sixteen years old, and she'd never been kissed. Katie was beginning to feel abnormal.

"Hey, K.C. Yoo-hoo!" Ted Mason called.

Katie looked away from the window and grinned at Ted, who had just walked into the activities room. The tall, dark-haired football captain stood against the wall next to her, looking as restless as she felt. Ted had been one of her secret crushes last fall. But he had been so in love with a lifeguard from California he had met over the summer, he hadn't looked at another girl all year. Recently the lifeguard, Molly Ramirez, had landed back in Rose Hill and she and Ted were blissfully reunited. Katie didn't feel at all bad about that. She'd only known the high-spirited Molly a couple of months now, but Katie counted her among her very best friends.

Looking past Ted's broad shoulders, Katie noticed that Chris and Greg had finally come in. Greg had settled down into one of the wooden chairs surrounding the long table that took up most of the room. He had his "I Sailed Chesapeake Bay" cap on his head. As he talked chummily to Marty Leonard, the tall basketball forward, he looked so relaxed and laid-back, Katie had a feeling that whatever this silly secret meeting was about, Greg wasn't worried about it in the least. But was it possible Chris hadn't confided in Greg? His laid-back, easy mood contrasted sharply with Chris's obvious nervousness. She was standing at the front of the room, talking rapidly to Sasha Jenkins, editor of the school paper, *The Red and the Gold*. Both girls looked extremely serious, and Chris's classically beautiful face was scrunched up with worry.

"Any idea what this mysterious meeting's all about?" Ted voiced the same question everyone had been asking all day long, ever since Principal Beeman's announcement during homeroom this morning instructing representatives of all the teams to attend an emergency meeting after school. For once, the Kennedy grapevine failed to provide even the vaguest hint as to what Chris Austin and Principal Beeman were up to.

Katie shook her head. "Beats me, but Chris

4

looks upset, doesn't she? I wonder why Greg doesn't. I sort of figured he'd know everything by now," she speculated.

Ted chuckled. "Believe me, Greg's as much in in the dark as you or me. If something's top secret, Chris Austin wouldn't divulge one bit of information. Not even to her *boyfriend*." Before Ted met Molly, he had dated Chris, and Ted seemed to know her better than anyone.

"Weird. Definitely weird!" A guy chimed in from the other side of Ted. Katie craned her neck and looked past Ted. Her inquiring gaze met the laughing green eyes of a guy she recognized but couldn't place right away. Under his Cardinals letter jacket, he was wearing a green sweat shirt. His blond hair was slicked back and his eyes were a bit red around the rims. Katie realized he must be Eric Shriver, boys' swim team captain. He was a lot cuter than the picture she had seen in *The Red and the Gold* and she wondered why she had never noticed him before.

Eric met her gaze directly and his wide-cheekboned face slowly lit up with a smile. He held out his hand toward Katie. "You must be Katie Crawford, the gymnast. I heard you pulled some pretty mean scores yesterday at the meet over at St. Mary's Prep. Congratulations."

"Thanks — I'm surprised you know about it. The exploits in the girls' gym are the best kept secret around the quad." Katie laughed and reached across Ted to pump Eric's hand ceremoniously. She felt a funny thrill go through her as she took his hand. It was warm to touch, and his handshake was firm and strong, just the way he looked: determined, and very upfront. Suddenly Katie realized she had been holding Eric's hand just a little too long. A hint of color rushed to her face, and she dropped his hand, and lowered her lashes so she wouldn't have to look Eric in the eye. Katie thought he gave her hand a final squeeze. She shyly glanced up at Eric again, but he wasn't looking at her. He was talking to Ted when Chris's gavel struck the podium, and she called the meeting to order.

"I'll make this meeting short — if not sweet," Chris said with visible anxiety. She leaned her elbows on the podium and pushed her long blond hair back behind her shoulders. As Chris looked around the room meeting each person's eyes in turn she said, "Principal Beeman asked me to gather you all together to tell you about last night's school board meeting."

"Not again!" someone grumbled as an audible groan rippled through the room. School board meetings generally resulted in a new, unwelcome set of rules and regulations for school activities. At last month's meeting the cheerleaders' outfits were voted too skimpy and revealing. At the next basketball game, all members of the pep squad — male and female — had turned up wearing ankle-length skirts and baggy turtleneck sweaters. The protest was covered in the local paper and there was even an editorial about the wholesomeness of cheerleading. The issue was mysteriously dropped by the school board shortly thereafter.

Chris held up her hand. "The bad news this time around has to do with money."

Katie swung her legs down from the windowsill and leaned forward to listen better to what Chris was about to say.

"The school board has determined that Kennedy's athletic programs should be more self-supporting. They want to encourage all the teams to do individual fund-raising — selling candy, T-shirts, and stuff like that. The sports that get the biggest draw and the most support will get the biggest part of the pie in terms of school funding."

"What!" Katie exclaimed, jumping to her feet. "That's crazy! All the big sports — football, baseball — already get enough money. The rest of us are barely surviving now. There's no way you're going to get people interested in gymnastics — "

"Or swimming!" Eric piped up and stepped forward a couple of paces.

"She's right!" Greg said. "The more popular sports are always going to draw the biggest crowds. Half the school doesn't even know about the smaller teams like crew."

Chris threw up her hands. "Listen, I don't like it, either. Nobody does."

Ted raised his hand with a gesture of exaggerated politeness. "Madame President, may I take the floor?"

Chris heaved another sigh. "Of course, Ted." She leaned back against the chalkboard and folded her arms across her chest.

"I'm not saying the school board's absolutely right about this. It seems like Rose Hill should have more than enough money to support all of Kennedy's sports," Ted said reasonably. "But it makes some sense that the sports that kids on campus don't support don't deserve as much com-

7

munity support. Besides, the "bigger" teams, like football, really need more money — our equipment costs a fortune."

"Ted Mason, how can you say a thing like that?" Katie declared. She marched up to the front of the room and planted her hands on her slender hips. Her dark brown eyes seemed to flash fire as she spoke. "I think Kennedy owes it to everybody, in school, around Rose Hill, to support those very sports that don't have a high profile. Of *course* a football or baseball game is more fun to go to than a gymnastics meet. It's a big social event! Can you imagine asking someone on a date to watch — " Katie looked around the room for inspiration. Her eyes settled on Eric. " — the boys' high-dive competition, or the butterfly race down at the pool? But that doesn't make the sport less important. Not at all." She turned to Chris and addressed her directly. "We're the ones who actually need *more* money from school funds — not less. How many people outside of this room — or inside for that matter — know that in two weeks the girls' gymnastics team might make it to the state finals for the first time in Kennedy's history?"

A chorus of cheers greeted Katie's announcement. Then she added, "But we barely have the money to get there," and the cheers turned to hisses.

Chris pounded the podium. "Listen, I don't make the policy around here. But it's up to each one of you to figure out what you and your teams can do about this problem." Chris paused to clear her throat. It was obvious she didn't like what

8

she had to say. "My job is getting together the figures, the statistics, and the attendance records for the past year. At the end of next week I have to present them to the school board, along with my recommendations for who gets what."

"You decide?" Greg said, amazed.

Chris met Greg's eyes steadily, then looked around the room. "And I promise to be fair and impartial and to do the best job I can to give every team its due. I really mean that," she said with great conviction.

Katie wasn't convinced. "I don't believe this," she muttered to herself, making her way past Ted and hoisting herself up on the windowsill. "That means crew will get everything, and the rest of us nothing. After all, he is her boyfriend!"

"K. C.," Ted whispered to her, "I told you, the one person I've ever met who never, and I mean *never*, would be partial to the guy she loves is Chris Austin. In fact, she'd probably bend over backward to be sure no one could accuse her of playing favorites."

Katie didn't answer. If she were in Chris's shoes, she knew she wouldn't be able to play fair. As Chris began to rattle off some nasty-sounding dollar figures and statistics, Katie crossed her legs and mentally calculated exactly what would happen in the next week. The big teams wouldn't be affected one way or another by Chris's decision. The little ones — her team, Eric's, Greg's, Tara Reese's ever-struggling track and field team, and all the others would have to fight tooth and nail to convince Chris and the school board that they were worth supporting.

9

From her perch on the windowsill, Katie sized up her competition. The five-feet-two gymnast looked first at Greg. Greg and his crew team had even less financial and student body support than girls' gymnastics. The problem was, she loved the idea of crew. The other day she'd overheard some girls in the locker room saying that Greg was trying to drum up support for a girls' crew team. Katie didn't like the idea of fighting with Greg over money. In fact, she didn't feel like fighting with anybody — Greg, Tara, or Eric.

She glanced over toward Eric and was startled to find him studying her intently. He sheepishly flashed her a victory sign and mouthed "Good show!" Eric motioned with his hand toward the door, and Katie figured he meant he wanted to talk to her later. She nodded and tried not to place too much importance on the fact that as soon as Chris finished up, Katie would get to talk to him alone. She was used to guys being friendly to her. She was a very friendly person herself and not in the least bit shy.

But the little thrill in her heart when she caught Eric looking at her just now made her wary. She felt another crush coming on, and she wasn't convinced that the start of a real battle to save the gymnastics team was a good time for her to get hooked on a guy who probably just wanted to talk funding crisis. Athlete-to-athlete. Pal-to-pal, as usual. Certainly not girl to guy. No, Katie Crawford wasn't at all ready for her fourth one-sided romance of junior year.

Chapter
2

"So Katie — alias K. C. Crawford — where do we go from here?" Eric asked as they clattered down the short flight of concrete steps behind the main building onto the sunny quad. The meeting had finally broken up. True to his word, Eric had waited for Katie in the hall, just outside the door.

Katie blinked. "Uh — I don't know," she said, taken aback by his question. She suddenly had this crazy feeling that Eric Shriver, far from being her fourth doomed crush of the year, was about to ask her on a date. She held her breath waiting for him to go on.

Eric seemed let down by her response. He hopped up on the black metal bike rack and balanced his books on one knee. "Well, if we don't come up with something, we might as well forget about having a swim or gymnastics team next year."

Katie's heart sank. She was right after all. Eric only wanted to talk to her about the funding crunch. A small sigh escaped her lips, but she pushed aside her own disappointment and cleared her throat. Whatever vibes she thought she was getting from Eric must be all in her mind. She took a deep breath and stood determined to talk to Eric as just another athlete, or as another new friend, rather than a boy in the "boyfriend" category. He was certainly right about the future of their teams being at stake. Katie shifted her new roller skates from her left shoulder to her right.

"I'm fresh out of brilliant ideas at the moment," she finally admitted, then looked up at Eric. He patted the railing next to him, motioning for Katie to sit down.

"Two minds sometimes work better than one." Eric grinned a disarmingly crooked grin and held Katie's glance.

Her heart started thumping. She cocked her head. Those mixed messages again. He was talking as if he wanted to just be her friend, but there seemed to be another conversation going on beneath the surface that had nothing to do with words, and everything to do with the way he was looking at her. Katie couldn't quite figure it out, but she leaned back against the rail right next to him. She was conscious of his strong, muscular body next to hers, and the faint, clean scent of chlorine coming from his hair. Being so near him made her feel a little dizzy, lightheaded, and airy inside — almost too spacey to talk.

But she surprised herself by sounding very sensible as she said, "Somehow, we've got to convince Chris in the next week or so that the minor sports aren't minor at all. After all," she concluded with an indignant sniff, "during the last Olympics it was the swimmers and gymnasts and track and field stars that got everyone so excited. Lots of them were high school kids just like us."

Eric nodded. He kicked a drift of cherry blossoms that had gathered around the base of the bike rack and looked over Katie's shoulders across the quad. After a moment's silence he cleared his throat, stretched his muscular arms over his head, and leaned back a little, lifting his face to the sun. "Sounds like we need to do some brainstorming," he said, casually bringing his glance back to Katie. He studied her intently, then asked, "How about talking things out over some pizza — I'm so starved my brain is on standby. I'll drive you home after — "

Katie's smile widened into a broad grin. "Oh, I'd love that!" she said eagerly, then her face fell. "But I can't. I've got a date." Seeing the disappointment register on Eric's face, she added quickly, "With my friend Molly — we're going roller-skating." She caught her breath slightly, as Eric reached across her shoulder and gave one of her roller skate wheels a playful spin. His hands were square and strong, and she had a terrible urge to touch them.

"Going roller-skating, are you?" He laughed. "Has Coach Gleason choreographed some cartwheels for you to do on skates?"

Katie giggled. "Now that's something I hadn't even thought of — yet. But it's a good idea. Maybe I'll try it."

"I hope you're kidding."

"Maybe, maybe not," she teased. Then she asked on impulse, "Do you skate?"

Eric eyed Katie's skates skeptically. "I haven't been on a pair of those since I was in grade school. My last pair are buried in the back of my closet — the plastic ones that you tighten with some kind of big blue plastic key." He scrunched up his face at the memory, and his slightly turned-up nose wrinkled pleasantly.

"Once you learn, it's something you never forget — like swimming. I'll give you a brush-up lesson sometime, if you like," Katie suggested, twirling the end of her bright blue skate lace around and around with her finger.

Eric grinned. "Hey, I'd like that. I'd really like that. But now," he said, shouldering his knapsack and stuffing his hands into his jacket pockets, "I'm off to feed my brain." He tapped his fist against his head and winked at Katie. Then, turning on his heels, he headed for the parking lot.

Katie watched him cross the grass toward the parking lot until he disappeared down the path winding behind the science building.

She stood there, staring at the space he left for a long time, unable to stop smiling and feeling a little shell-shocked. He had really offered to drive her home. All those little looks, those accidental touches, maybe for once they really meant something! With all her heart, Katie hoped they did. Because if someone had asked her to describe her dream boy, Eric would fit the bill perfectly. Not too tall. Not too short. Strong, with green

14

eyes, a great laugh, and a deep dimple in one cheek when he smiled.

With a happy sigh, she dropped down to the grass and put on her skates. She whistled the Kennedy fight song as she laced up her black high-topped boot. The whistle abruptly died on her lips, and a small wrinkle worked its way across her forehead. Katie looked up and stared across the quad to the place where Eric had been. Was she crazy? Eric had wanted to talk about the funding crisis over pizza. That was all. When she couldn't go along, he headed straight for the pizza place anyway, and here she was acting as if he had asked her out on a date. If he were really interested, something else would have happened. He could have hung around until Molly turned up. Or he could have made a definite date to go skating. After all, tomorrow *was* Saturday. But he hadn't suggested a skating date even though she had given him that opening. She had mentioned being willing to teach him, but he hadn't quite responded the way she would have liked. Not really. Not like a guy who was dying to go out with her. Katie let out a disappointed sigh and sat listlessly on the grass holding one skate in her hand, wondering if she would ever get guys' signals straight. Especially guys she really liked. Like Eric Shriver.

Molly Ramirez found Katie like that, one skate off, one skate on, staring ruefully toward the parking lot as if she had just lost her best friend.

"Katie Crawford! You look like a kitten who just lost her mitten. What's with you, buddy?"

15

Molly spun around on her skates, and toed to a halt.

"Uh, nothing," Katie lied and hurriedly jammed her foot into her skate.

"Nothing, my eye!" Molly said knowingly. She propped herself against the bike rack and began retying the red-and-black polka-dot scarf in her thick, curly ponytail. "I saw you with that hunk Eric Shriver just now."

"You what?" Katie gulped and scrambled to her feet, almost losing her balance. She dusted off her faded jeans and faced Molly head on. "You know him?" she sputtered. "Since when?"

"Of course, I know him," Molly said, waving her hand toward the parking lot. Then she peered shrewdly at Katie. "I bet I've known him longer than you," she teased in a childishly singsong voice. She managed to keep a straight face, but her huge blue eyes glinted mischievously as she said, "In fact, I'd say Eric Shriver is probably one of the best kissers I've ever met — with the exception of Ted, of course."

"What!" Katie wailed, indignant. "How do you know that?"

Molly doubled over with laughter, and skated backward toward the concrete steps leading up to the back entrance to the school. She sat down and wiped a tear off her cheek. "So, you really are interested in him." She gasped and began laughing again as Katie protested.

"Would you stop that? I've never even met Eric before today, and who said I'm interested in him, anyway? You're jumping to conclusions, Molly."

16

"Well," Molly managed finally, "I was going to tell you all about it, anyway."

Katie skated over and joined her on the steps. She tied on her knee guards and waited for Molly to stop giggling long enough to tell her story.

"The other day I was giving a lifesaving demonstration for the swim team. Eric was the first to volunteer for mouth-to-mouth resuscitation. He dove in the pool and pretended to drown. I jumped in after him, hauled him out — let me tell you, he's not very tall, but he weighs a ton. He's sooooo strong!" She rolled her eyes expressively and made her arm bulge into a muscle.

"And then what happened?" Katie asked.

"I got him all stretched out on the side of the pool, and began demonstrating the mouth-to-mouth, and would you believe it — he grabbed me and began really kissing me!"

"What!" Katie cried, and squinted toward the parking lot. "What did you do about it?" she asked, planting her hands on her hips and looking Molly squarely in the eye.

Molly shrugged. "What could I do?" She paused for a tantalizing moment. Then her face softened as she looked at Katie. "You really like him, don't you?" she murmured.

Katie didn't seem to hear.

So Molly continued with her tale. "I flipped him right back in the pool, and I bet his back really smarted when he hit the water."

Katie began to chuckle. "You're crazy, Ramirez. You really are. I'm glad you've got a boyfriend, 'cause you're such a flirt. I bet you enjoyed that kiss before you tossed him in."

Molly gave a noncommital little grunt. "The best part was everyone — even old stoneface Coach Smithson — really cracked up." Molly started laughing again, then said ruefully, "I *didn't* enjoy facing Ted afterward."

"Ted was there?" Katie asked, confused.

"No. But word got around by the time I hit the sub shop that afternoon. Ted was livid. I think he was about to pick a fight with Eric until Eric finally explained. He really didn't know Ted and I were going together. Lots of people don't yet. Ted was okay about it in the end. He asked Eric to join us at Rosemont Park tomorrow for the softball game."

"Eric's coming to the game?" Katie exclaimed, her face lighting up. Maybe that was why he didn't ask her to go skating tomorrow.

Molly studied her friend a moment. "He's a real nice guy, Katie. And he's not attached. Marc Harrison mentioned that the other night. I could see you two together. I really could."

"Come off it!" Katie protested, trying to wipe the grin off her face and failing miserably. "I hardly know him. And besides, you know my batting average with guys is .000 percent at this point."

"I have a feeling things are about to change," Molly said, getting up and beginning to skate down the path. "Eric's different than the other guys you liked this year. He's not at all like that baseball player, and then that other one, the guy who works with Jeremy Stone on the yearbook. Harold whatever who looks like your basic hunk with no brains. You never did tell me who the third guy was, but he was pretty dumb, too, not to like you."

And Katie wouldn't tell Molly, either. Molly might feel weird that once upon a time Katie had had a crush on Ted. As they skated down the back roads toward the mall and the ice-cream parlor, she hung back a little behind her friend. Now that she had met Eric, every other guy she had liked paled by comparison. Even good-natured Ted.

Katie's new skates fit perfectly, but she hardly noticed. Her mind wasn't on the traffic, or Molly's pleasant chattering about school and the upcoming weekend. She was only thinking about Eric, and how perfect it would be to see him again tomorrow. Knowing he didn't have a girl friend renewed Katie's confidence. Maybe Eric hadn't meant anything romantic by asking her for pizza, but maybe he had. Why should she choose the gloomy scenario? She might as well think that he had wanted to be alone with her, to get to know her better, not just to share a pizza, or their interest in a good cause. If you didn't go into a game imagining you would win it, then you'd probably lose. Loss, defeat, giving up — those words had never existed in Katie's vocabulary before all these confusing experiences with guys. Well, she was going to erase them once and for all now.

"WATCH OUT!" Molly screeched, grabbing Katie's arm. Katie had practically skated into the flag pole at the entrance to the mall.

"Thanks," Katie managed to say, a bit shaken. Molly shook her head knowingly. "You're pretty far gone over Eric. And don't you try to deny it."

Katie was about to anyway, then changed her mind. "Who's denying anything? After all, spring has sprung and just about anything wonderful can happen. Don't you feel it, Molly? Winning meets, going to the states, and giving the school board some facts and figures they're going to be embarrassed about. Anything can happen," she said, leading the way to the mall entrance nearest Sticky Fingers. Under her breath, sure that Molly couldn't hear, she added "even love." With that, she crossed her fingers and rolled onto the rubber mat, triggering open the sliding glass automated door.

Chapter
3

"Greg," Chris murmured into the soft collar of her boyfriend's knit polo shirt. "Everyone can see us!" she feebly pushed her hands against his chest. Kissing in the front seat of Greg's mother's white Mercedes in the middle of the afternoon outside the sub shop wasn't exactly Chris Austin's idea of proper behavior.

Not that she was feeling very proper at the moment. Holding Greg like this tended to muddle Chris's clearheaded thought processes. Part of her was wondering if she had ever loved anyone this much in her whole life. Part of her wanted to skip going to the sub shop entirely and drive out to the country. Out to a magically secluded spot she had found last year with her old boyfriend, Ted Mason, during a class picnic. There was a winding path leading up behind the Maryville Theatre into a state forest. The wild cherries would have blossomed by now, and the afternoon was still warm. Along the path there was a beautiful little cave that looked as if it were inhabited by gnomes or fairies. Ted had carved their initials there last year. Now she wanted to carve Greg's name next to hers. But Chris knew she wouldn't even hint at going for a ride. Greg would jump at the chance to drive out to Maryville, and Chris's folks would kill her if she were late for dinner. Besides, she had a ton of homework this weekend, as well as those awful sports attendance statistics to get together for the school board. Then she and Greg were supposed to go up to Lost Lake the next afternoon to try out Greg's new sailboat, the one he had gotten for his sixteenth birthday.

Chris sighed and pillowed her cheek against Greg's chest. Being alone with Greg would have to wait until tomorrow. "We really shouldn't be doing this," she whispered without much conviction.

"Who's looking? Besides — who cares?" Greg released his hold on her slightly and glanced past Chris's shoulder through the windshield. Except for a woman pushing a stroller in front of the card shop next door to the popular Kennedy hangout, the sidewalk was deserted. Jukebox music filtered out of the open double doors into the parking lot. Anyone who cared about what Greg or Chris did was already celebrating Friday, the weekend, and the strong, heady feeling of spring in the air. "Besides, this is a special occasion — me being able to drive *you* somewhere for a change!" Greg said happily. As Greg tilted Chris's face up toward his, his blue-green eyes crinkled with laughter. He was obviously pleased with him-

22

self. The tall Kennedy sophomore had recently turned sixteen and had gotten his driver's license a few days ago. Until then, one of the in-jokes among the crowd had been how Chris was always in the driver's seat in this relationship. Greg had good-humoredly laughed along, though now and then it got to him. He couldn't help being two years younger than the popular student body president. But after months of their going together, some factions around school still made a big deal out of their age difference.

"Well, then," Chris said slowly, a wicked glint lighting up her blue eyes, "since no one is watching, I guess one more kiss won't hurt. After all, you did chauffeur me safely the whole mile-and-a-half from school." She wrapped her arms around his neck and kissed him gently on the lips, then responded more passionately as he ran his fingers through her silky blond hair and pulled her closer.

They were still lost in their embrace when a somewhat out-of-tune chorus of "Hail to the Chief" led by Woody Webster started up. Chris and Greg sprang apart, but not before Woody reached inside the rolled-down window and yanked open Greg's door.

"Here he is, the president-napper himself!" Woody scrunched up his expressive face in a look of great horror. "Naughty, naughty!" He waved his finger under Greg's nose, as the tall, leggy sophomore scrambled out of the car. "The Secret Service will be after you! Seducing the president of Kennedy High in broad daylight. That brings *very* severe penalties, you know."

"Watch it, Webster!" Greg warned, snapping

Woody's trademark red suspenders sharply. "Or you're going to experience some severe penalties yourself!"

Chris hurriedly tucked her shirt back into her khaki pants, and hopped out of her side of the car. She was blushing furiously. Kim Barrie gave her arm a friendly pat and Chris started giggling. Standing behind Kim was the student activities director, Jonathan Preston. Jonathan's girl friend, Fiona Stone, was kneeling in the front seat of Jonathan's pink Chevy convertible, fixing her makeup in the rearview mirror. Apparently Woody and his contingent had just arrived at the sub shop themselves.

"Hey, aren't you supposed to be in the driver's seat?" Fiona said in her clipped British accent. She looked from Chris to Greg. "I mean, Greg can't drive yet, can he?"

"Yes he can. As of yesterday," Chris answered, sounding very proud.

"I actually got here in one piece." Greg laughed as he led the crowd into the sub shop.

"That's good, because if anything happened to Chris there'd be some serious consequences," Woody stated solemnly. "For instance, you'd look like the missing half of a matched set!" With an eloquent gesture Woody directed everyone's attention to Chris and Greg's matching outfits. A couple of months ago Chris and Greg had started dressing alike once in a while. Today they both wore navy-blue Polo shirts, khaki pants, and topsiders.

Marc Harrison and Dee Patterson were already at the crowd's favorite table — the sub shop's coveted booth situated in a corner near the moth-eaten stuffed bear, the restaurant's mascot. Chris walked over to them and claimed the corner seat by the wall. Dee was delicately nibbling a lettuce leaf claimed from her boyfriend's Heroic Hollywood Ham sub. She looked up and smiled warmly at Chris.

"What took you so long?" Marc asked Chris. He had been at the sports meeting representing the soccer team and had seen Chris leave with Greg as soon as the meeting broke up.

Chris colored slightly, but said airily, "Greg drove me. You know how long it takes new drivers to get anywhere."

"He got his license!" Dee clapped. "Good for you, Montgomery!" She smiled as the sandy-haired sophomore deposited a Coke and a salad in front of Chris, and a Super Salami Sinker Sub in front of his own place. Woody and the other kids followed close on his heels.

Greg bowed formally from the waist and patted himself on the back. "Aw — it was nothing!" he said modestly, making a big show of jingling the car keys in his hand.

"Is that *your* Mercedes out there?" Marc mumbled through a mouthful of his sandwich.

Chris laughed. "It's his mom's."

"They asked me if I wanted a car for my birth-day, but I wanted a boat more. You should see my new sailboat. It's great. We're going to try it tomorrow up at Lost Lake. Anyone want to come?"

"Tomorrow?" Woody shook his head ruefully. "Tomorrow's the big softball game in Rosemont

Park. I was counting on you two being there." He pulled a crumpled sheet of loose leaf paper out of his shirt pocket and ran his finger down a penciled list of names. Kim looked over his shoulder, and began counting players.

"There are still enough for almost two full teams," she said, then turned to Chris and Greg, "Not that we won't miss both of you."

Chris pushed a stray wisp of blond hair off her cheek and wrinkled her nose. "I hate missing it, but I really am in the mood to get up into the mountains. Jeremy and Diana are coming with us. Anyone else is welcome. Still, if I could be in two places at the same time. . . ." Chris felt funny missing the first ballgame of the year. For three years now, she and her crowd had always gathered in the park for a formal "Welcome to Spring" softball match. But the weather promised to be perfect for sailing, and Greg was dying to try out his new boat.

"Speaking of boats," Marc interjected. "That school board decision sure is going to rock a few boats in Kennedy's athletic program." Marc was on the soccer team. Like Ted, he was pretty sure his team wouldn't be adversely affected by anything Chris decided in the way of funding allocations.

Chris groaned, propping her forehead in her hands. "I don't want to talk about it. I feel like I've been put right in the middle of a Ms. Unpopularity contest, and I'm headed straight for the winner's circle. I thought Katie Crawford was going to kill me."

"It's not your fault you have to decide, though

I don't exactly know why the student body president has to be so involved. It's tough on you," Fiona commented sympathetically. "It's not fair. You're everyone's friend — most of the captains of the sports involved know you real well." Fiona gave a meaningful glance toward Greg.

Greg put his arm around Chris and patted her shoulder. "Don't worry, Chris will play fair." After a pause he added with a wriggle of his eyebrows, "Of course, crew does deserve a big piece of the pie. You've got to admit it's the hottest new program at Kennedy."

"Come off it!" Marc countered. You've got ten members on the team. Half of Kennedy doesn't even know we have a crew team."

"But they will after this spring," Greg said staunchly. "We're going to make a big splash — "

Woody moaned over Greg's pun.

Greg continued without missing a beat. " — as long as our boats don't sink." Thanks to Greg's formidable business savvy and salesmanship, he had obtained a donation of two very used but flexible eight-oared shells from Georgetown University. With the help of a couple of volunteers from Matt Jacob's Fix-It Club, he had gotten one boat in working order before the fall practice season was over. He had whipped up eight rowers and a coxswain and lined up races scheduled to begin at the end of the month with a couple of the Washington area's most prestigious high school crew teams: Leesburg and Potomac Prep. Greg was practical enough to know that his fledgling team didn't stand a chance of winning against practiced, well-drilled rowers who had been work-

27

ing shoulder to shoulder with each other through-out their high school careers. But by the start of next year's competitive season, if funds weren't cut, he was certain that next year the Cardinals' crew would have a chance at winning the local junior division championship.

"Leave it to a Montgomery not to worry about a little detail like money!" Marc laughed.

"Why should he?" Jonathan joked, shoving his felt Indiana Jones hat back on his head and regarding Greg with laughing gray eyes. He cast a significant glance in Chris's direction. "He's got an in, don't you know?" he said, mimicking Fiona's British accent.

Chris gulped. "What do you mean by that?" she said sharply.

"Come off it, Chris," Dee said. "Don't tell me you don't remember our history teacher's recent lecture on nepotism. You know, when kings or prime ministers or presidents hand out favors to close relatives."

"Greg's not a relative of Chris's," Fiona stated, looking a bit blank.

"That, my dear, is all relative!" Woody punned, and reached across the table to playfully punch Greg's shoulder. "He's pretty close to it."

"Are you suggesting that I'd favor Greg?" Chris asked, horrified. She sat up very straight and turned to Greg, waiting for him to deny Jonathan's accusation outright.

Greg considered Chris a moment, then his smile widened into a grin. "Not a bad idea! Why didn't I think of it first?" He leaned back in his

28

seat, propping his elbows against the top of the chair, and winked at Chris. "Let's go outside and talk about this somewhere where no one can hear us," he whispered loudly across the table, gesturing to the back door.

Chris's lips drew into a thin narrow line, and she glared at her boyfriend. A second later, Greg, then Woody, then everyone except Chris, cracked up.

"You think I'm serious!" Greg said, wiping tears of laughter from his cheeks. Chris eyed Greg suspiciously, then the tiny hint of a smile began to cross her face.

She shrugged and looked around the table. "I guess I was so surprised by everyone even thinking I'd play favorites, I got a little too serious."

"That's why we love you!" Dee smiled warmly. "You didn't get elected president because you were a stand-up comic, Chris."

Woody pounded the table, making everyone jump slightly. "But Chris has every right to be serious," he declared solemnly. He looked surreptitiously around the room and beckoned everyone at the booth to lean in close around the table. "This is a most utterly serious matter!"

"Woody!" Chris began to protest. For a second there she had begun to enjoy the joke but now she wished Woody would just drop it.

"If there is the remotest suspicion a particular tall sophomore and his watery cohorts got one penny more than they deserved — "

"Stop it, Woody!" Chris complained edgily.

Woody just ignored her. "There's going to be

a Kennedy High equivalent of a House Sub-Committee investigation of alleged widespread corruption in student government!"

Through gritted teeth Chris forced a smile, but she began nervously drumming her fingers against the worn wooden boards of the bench. What were Woody and Jonathan hinting at? Were they really joking?

As talk finally turned back to tomorrow's softball game, Chris leaned back in her seat and stared over Kim's head into the dusty, once-glimmering glass eyes of the stuffed bear. Chris thoughtfully gnawed the inside of her lip and wondered. Until this very second she had never thought of herself as a person capable of being unfair. Almost against her will, she found her gaze shifting toward Greg. He was sitting next to her, talking avidly with Woody about whether Molly Ramirez or Elise Hammond would make a better shortstop.

As always, just looking at Greg's handsome profile sent a chill from the ends of Chris's toes clear up her spine. It was all she could do not to reach out and push a stray bit of Greg's sandy hair back behind his ear. His boundless enthusiasm for starting the first crew team at Kennedy was contagious. Kids who had never even heard of competitive boat-racing were now among the best rowers he had. Chris wanted more than anything for the crew team to succeed, especially now that Greg was training a couple of sophomore girls who were interested in coxing for his girls' team.

But what if crew proved too exclusive? Chris

had no figures yet, but she suddenly doubted that Greg's team would benefit from any funding changes. In fact, its very future might be threatened. They hadn't even had a race yet. Student body support probably didn't exist. After this spring season, by next fall, kids would be all excited about it. But now. . . .

Chris slouched down in her seat and looked away from Greg. How could she face him if she had to decide crew was the team to get the most cuts? He'd be so hurt.

On the other hand, what if she, even unconsciously, weighted the odds in his favor, as Jonathan and Woody suggested she would. Then she wouldn't be able to face herself, either. For the first time since she had taken office as student body president, Chris Austin hated her job with a passion.

That night, Chris padded down the hall from the bathroom and paused outside her stepsister's door. A trickle of light seeped from beneath it, cutting a path across the dark blue carpet.

It was past midnight, but in spite of a long, hot bath followed by a steamy shower, Chris wasn't the least bit sleepy. She was nervous, worried, and upset, and needed someone to talk to. Someone she could trust to tell the truth — no matter how unpleasant the truth may be. Chris wrapped her long, pink terry robe more closely around her, rubbed a tense spot on the back of her neck, and knocked very softly on Brenda's door. She waited a second, then walked in.

Brenda was lying on her back on the bed with

31

her head dangling over the side, her long dark hair almost brushing the white shag carpet. She was still dressed in her black jeans and oversized gray cotton sweater. The phone was balanced on top of her stomach, and Brenda's delicate hand was resting on the receiver. From the dreamy expression on Brenda's face, Chris knew her sister had been talking to her boyfriend Brad. Brad was a first-year pre-med student at Princeton, but in a few weeks he'd be back home for the summer. Chris knew Brenda was counting the days, hours, minutes, and seconds until his return.

Chris stood in the doorway of the comfortably cluttered bedroom, waiting for Brenda to notice her. But her sister didn't stir on the bed and, after a moment's silence, Chris cleared her throat and said, "Uh, Bren, you busy?"

Brenda snapped out of her dreamy state and sat up straight on the bed, looking a little embarrassed. "Sorry. I didn't realize you had come in." She put the phone back on her night table, stood up, and stretched. She rolled her neck a couple of times, and the large silver hoop earrings sparkled against the olive skin of her neck. When she straightened up, she glanced more carefully at Chris, her doelike brown eyes filling with concern. "Hey, you look like you need to talk," she said, patting the foot of her bed and sitting down again. Brenda's work with problem teens at Garfield House, a halfway house in Georgetown, had made her extra-sensitive to other kids' moods. Over the past year or so she had become Chris's chief confidante, outside of Phoebe Hall. Chris nodded, took a deep breath, kicked off her slippers and plopped down on top of Brenda's black-and-gray bedspread.

"It's about Greg," Chris started slowly, running her finger over a circular pattern woven into the spread.

"Did you have a fight?"

"No," Chris said with an abrupt toss of her head. She pulled her hair back from her face and began braiding it. Brenda knelt behind her and said, "Here, let me."

As Chris talked, Brenda swiftly plaited her sister's hair in a single long braid.

After another deep breath, Chris continued. "It's about this dumb funding crisis and the school board, and the fact that Greg is on the crew team." Chris paused and stared at her hands. She clenched and unclenched the broad terry tie of her robe. She looked over her shoulder, and her eyes, as they sought Brenda's, were dark with worry.

"Brenda, everyone's saying I can't be fair about who gets what funds. That I'll fix the figures, or — oh, I don't know — " She broke off, finding it hard to repeat Jonathan's words. Brenda waited until Chris finally said in a low, uncertain voice, "Jonathan even said I'd be sure to favor crew over the other teams. And — and, somehow, I think Greg expects me to do that." Her voice sank almost to a whisper. "I feel horrible. Just horrible. I can't believe that people think I'd act like that. And I have the awful feeling this whole crisis is going to affect my relationship with Greg.

I'm so scared." Brenda's room was warm, but Chris gave a little shiver and clutched her robe more tightly around her.

Brenda responded instantly. "Oh, Chris! Don't be ridiculous. Everyone knows you wouldn't do something like that. I'm sure Jonathan was just kidding — "

"Of course he was kidding," Chris interrupted. "I know that. But still, it's the principle of the thing." Chris jumped to her feet and began pacing back and forth in front of Brenda's cluttered desk. "If my friends think like that — what will everyone else think?"

"Christine Austin!" Brenda said sharply. "Stop worrying about what people think. *That's* where you really start getting into trouble. Just do what's fair. You don't have an unfair bone in your body." Brenda sighed. Chris was the most "perfect" person she'd ever met. In fact, Chris's perfection used to drive Brenda crazy until she began to understand her overachieving sister. Chris was a born competitor, a born winner, with a great sense of fair play. She was honest and upfront and loyal by nature. Over the nearly two years since Brenda had gotten to know her, she had seen Chris and her flaws, just like anyone else. But generally, she was one of the most trustworthy people Brenda had ever encountered.

Chris pondered Brenda's words a moment, then flopped down again on the bed. "I hope you're right," she said, burying her face in Brenda's pillow. "I'm going to try my hardest not to be influenced. I just hope when I get those figures together, crew doesn't turn out to be the one small team with the biggest draw, and the most student support. No one will ever believe I didn't cheat to help the guy I love."

Brenda replied instantly with great conviction. "I'll believe it. Phoebe will believe it. Everyone who really knows you, Chris, knows you couldn't cheat a soul. Period."

The beginning of a smile appeared on Chris's face. The tense knot in the back of her neck seemed to loosen a little. "I guess what really matters is that I do the best job I can gathering the information for the school board. I can't help but be fair doing that." She sat back on her heels and nodded thoughtfully. How silly she had been today, making mountains out of mole hills as usual. The funding crunch *was* a pretty sticky situation, and with all her heart Chris didn't want *anyone's* budget cut — not Greg's, Katie's, Tara's. She had firmly argued her point with Mr. Beeman before today's meeting. Rose Hill was too prosperous a community to have to play such silly games with school money. But the school board controlled the purse strings, and Chris was powerless against their decision, irrational as it seemed.

Chris had a job to do, and she was determined to do her best at it as usual, even if the circumstances weren't quite "as usual" for the fair-minded Kennedy student leader. Nothing involving Greg was ever "as usual" for Chris. She had changed since she had met him. Knowing Greg had made her more daring, more confident in taking chances, and freer and looser.

In Greg, Chris had finally found someone who didn't criticize her for her beliefs, her principles, or her passion for doing the right thing, however difficult the situation. Greg was just like her that way. And knowing that gave Chris a kind of courage, daring, and freedom to sometimes do the unexpected. No wonder Jonathan had made that offhanded remark today. Some girls *would* favor their guys — but Chris Austin wasn't quite like any other girl. Greg understood that better than anyone. She'd be extra careful to play fair this time around. Besides, she was sure Greg was right when he had said the crew team had nothing to worry about. He wouldn't expect her to cheat. He just believed in the worth of his team, and like every other good team captain, was convinced his team would come up deserving more than a small share of the pie.

Chris slipped off Brenda's bed. She gave her sister a hug and headed across the hall to her own bedroom, her fingers crossed in her bathrobe pockets. She whispered a wish as she turned back the satiny blue quilt. "Please, let Greg be right about his team," she said, climbing into bed and flicking off her light.

Chapter
4

Saturday afternoon Eric Shriver stood on the pitcher's mound trying to keep his eye on the plate and off the small, red-pigtailed figure crouching in the batter's box. She was supposed to be the opposition, the "Hill Street Blues" shortstop, and his second out of the inning. But to Eric she was the girl he'd just lost half a night's sleep over: Katie Crawford. She was certainly the last person in the world he wanted to strike out.

With his left hand behind his back, Eric shifted the softball around, feeling for the seams. But his mind wasn't on the seams or his next pitch, but on Katie, and the warm challenging smile she had flashed him when she walked up to the plate.

"PLAY BALLLLLLL!" Woody Webster shouted from behind home plate. "Let's go, Shriver. First you show up late, and now you're holding up the whole game!"

"I'm trying, I'm trying," Eric mumbled to himself, then sighed.

He shoved his baseball cap back on his head and grinned toward home plate. "K.C.," he shouted, suddenly inspired to throw her an easy pitch. After all, his team was winning, and Katie looked so small and vulnerable out there. "See if you can hit this one," he said with a smile. He aimed the ball and threw it right in the strike zone.

WHACK came the solid connection of wood against the softball. The ball shot like a bullet far over Eric's head. He whirled around on the mound, half expecting the ball to soar to the outfield and into Marc Harrison's waiting glove. Eric had wanted Katie to hit it, but not like that. The ball kept going, past Marc, past the boundaries of the field, and finally landed out near the tennis courts.

Eric doffed his cap and scratched his head, amazed. "I don't believe it!" he cried, as Katie whooped, tossed aside her bat and began circling the bases. "You're strong!" he exclaimed as she plopped one foot squarely down in the center of the second base bag.

Katie arched her eyebrows and shrugged. "Of course!" She smiled matter-of-factly, rounding second, and heading toward third.

"Hey, Shriver, don't look so shocked!" Peter Lacey shouted, pushing his catcher's mask on top of his dark wavy hair. His green eyes were shining as he jogged up to the mound. "Didn't you know her dad's a scout for the Orioles? He's a pro; he was a triple-A outfielder for a while. Katie's been playing ball since she was a kid."

38

Eric stared at Peter in dismay and suddenly realized he didn't know the first thing about Katie Crawford.

Peter chuckled and slapped Eric on the back. "Besides, even my six-year-old cousin could have whacked that one. You couldn't have given her a better pitch if you tried. If I didn't know you better, I'd swear you were trying to give her an easy run. Right down the middle. Vooom!" Peter thumped his fist in his mitt and gave Eric a puzzled look before jogging back to the plate. And no wonder — Eric had managed to strike out five Blues in a row before Katie came to bat. Suddenly he felt very embarrassed and vaguely annoyed. Everyone — including Katie — must have figured out why he'd thrown an easy pitch.

Eric's head snapped back toward Katie. She was at the Blues bench energetically slapping everyone five: Karen Davis, Kim, Molly, Brian Pierson, Ted, Ben Forrest, Jonathan, Fiona — everyone on her team. Now the Hill Street Blues trailed the Rosebuds by only one run.

"Pull yourself together, Shriver!" Monica Ford barked from first base. "Let's get going. I'm starved. I want to start the picnic part."

"Me, too," Brenda shouted from third.

Eric forced himself to stop staring at Katie, and put all his attention on striking out Ted, who was up next. Ted was the best hitter on both teams. Eric had his work cut out for him, but he hadn't been a champion Little League pitcher for nothing, he reminded himself. He wound up and hurled the softball.

"STRIIIIIIIIIIKE ONE!" Woody bellowed

39

and did a comical softshoe routine behind the plate. Instantly some kids from Garfield House, who were watching from the stands, gave Woody a big Bronx cheer.

"This is Saturday-afternoon softball, not *Saturday Night Live!*" Tony Martinez, the halfway house youth counselor, shouted from behind the Rosebud bench. A chorus of cheers and hoots greeted his remark.

Woody shrugged sheepishly, made a big business of squatting down behind Peter Lacey and cried once again, "PLAY BALL!"

Eric exhaled sharply, and allowed himself a small, triumphant smile, before his face grew serious. He fixed his attention back on the plate. Ted was a tough "out." But Eric had his pride on the line here, and his team was now in the lead by only one run. For the first time in twenty-four hours, he managed not to think of Katie or her smile or how strange and happy and a little confused it made him feel to see she was probably as good at baseball as he was.

By the bottom of the ninth, Eric was really sweating. Katie wasn't as good as he was. She was better. Eric was throwing his best stuff, but couldn't quite remember ever pitching to anyone back in Little League who could spot the perfect pitch so easily. He had a fleeting thought that if girls played pro baseball, Katie would make the majors. She was the last batter up. The count was three balls, two strikes, and there was a runner at first. Katie represented the winning run.

Knowing she might be coming to bat soon had

thrown Eric, because somehow, of all people, the
absolutely nonsports-oriented Fiona Stone had hit
his first pitch: a little looper that dropped to the
right of second base between Monica and Matt
Jacobs. When Woody told Fiona to run, the
pretty British ballerina looked very confused. She
started explaining she thought a run meant that
you hit the ball over toward the tennis courts,
but she made it to first base just in time.

Eric took a deep breath and relaxed his shoulders. He reached down and tossed his best pitch,
but it wasn't good enough. It was the same pitch
he'd struck Ted out with, but Katie had it timed
perfectly. She held back just long enough, then
walloped it deep into left field past Sasha Jenkins.
By the time Sasha hitched up her skirt, held her
wide-brimmed straw hat with one hand, and made
a valiant effort to chase down the ball, it was
already over the fence, and the Blues had won.

The minute she crossed homeplate, Katie vanished into a cheering throng of Blues and Rosebuds. She was the hero of the day, and everyone
knew it. Eric stood at the outskirts of the crowd,
his hat shoved back on his head, looking amazed.
Except for that one easy pitch to Katie in the
bottom of the seventh, he knew he had done his
best. As the crowd broke up, and headed for the
picnic area, his eyes were filled with admiration.
Not many guys he knew could hit a pitch like
that — so hard and so far. Eric walked up to her,
a congratulatory hand outstretched.

"What a run! You're great. You're really
great," he said, holding her hand a bit longer
than necessary. Eric dropped it when he saw the

41

blush rise to her cheeks, which were already pink from running.

"Thanks," Katie said, looking him directly in the eye. She cocked her head to the side and considered Eric carefully. "That was some pitch. You're really good, too." Katie looked down at her feet, and kicked some sand over the already half rubbed-out lines marking the batter's box.

"Except . . ." Katie continued, looking back into Eric's eyes, "after that pitch you tossed me back in the seventh, I thought my eight-year-old cousin Marcy could pitch better than you."

Eric flushed crimson. He gulped and tossed his glove from hand to hand. "Well, I didn't know — " he stammered. I — uh — didn't know you played ball so well. I thought that because you were — "

"A girl?" Katie supplied wickedly, then burst into a loud, hearty laugh. "You thought I'd need a little help?" She waved a scolding finger in his face.

Eric stood there, baffled a moment, and scratched his head. Katie's hand shot out to his arm, and she gave him a reassuring squeeze. "I'm just kidding," she said quickly, her mouth turning up into a soft, sweet smile. "I've got lots of brothers. I'm used to guys knowing I play games as hard as they do, I guess. We — " Katie said haltingly, "we don't know each other very well yet, do we?"

On impulse, Eric reached out and very gently rubbed a smudge of dust off Katie's cheek. "Well, let's do something about that," he said, dropping his hand to his side and keeping his eyes fixed on hers. They stood like that a moment. It was Katie who turned away first. She went over to the bench to retrieve her glove and jacket. Eric busied himself stuffing the balls at the base of the backstop into a gray canvas sack Woody had tossed behind homeplate.

"Hey, you two, you're just who I wanted to see." Katie and Eric both looked up. Karen Davis was standing at the plate holding a hot dog in one hand and her reporter's notebook under her arm. Despite playing nine innings of softball, the stunningly beautiful black girl looked perfectly cool in her spotless lemon-yellow sweats.

Katie glanced down at her own pink pin-striped pants. They were filthy. They hadn't been the most practical thing to play ball in, but they looked great with the pink bowling shirt she had picked up the week before at a flea market. Anyway, she had wanted to look great today, not sensible. The way Eric had touched her just now had proved her instincts about him were right. She blushed at the thought and awkwardly dusted off the side of her leg as she said, "Hi, Karen."

Karen was Sasha Jenkins' top reporter for *The Red and the Gold* as well as the news half of *News/Notes*, WKND's combination news and new music show. Karen had won a contest — actually *half* a contest — back in February. Cute, new music freak Brian Pierson had tied with her for first place. The prize was sharing a coveted new time slot on Kennedy's radio station. Their quirky combo show had become an instant hit. Karen's sharp interviews and inspired reporting had become one of the most listened-to half-hours

43

on the station. Brian's music contribution already had something of a cult following, on and off the quad. He'd even been written up in a local radio column. Word around campus was that Karen and Brian made quite a team, on air and off.

Karen took a bite of her hot dog and motioned toward the picnic table. "Aren't you guys starved?" She looked from Eric to Katie and smiled.

"We're going over the play-by-play. I think Katie needs to give me a couple of pitching pointers," Eric said smoothly, flashing Katie an easy smile.

Katie was surprised by how calm he sounded. Her own heart was pounding. All at once she knew that Eric wasn't half as flustered as she was. He was used to girls.

"I wanted to talk to you guys. I just wish Greg and Tara were here, too." She scanned the area as if the captains of the crew team and girls' track and field were lurking somewhere in the midst of the colorful crowd of Rose Hill families, joggers, and dog walkers.

"Greg's sailing somewhere, I heard," Eric said.

Karen giggled. "Makes sense. Well, I'll catch him Monday. Sasha and I had a long talk about Chris's meeting yesterday. I'm concerned about the funding crunch, and I'd like to help you all. I'd hate to see any team have their funds cut right now, especially you little guys. I'm thinking of doing an on-air editorial next week and getting some extra coverage of your events in the paper. Sasha agrees, and she's going to assign reporters to all your meets and workouts next week."

"Great!" Katie exclaimed. "If you could just put us on the map. Half the kids don't even know girls' gymnastics exists. The ones who do, don't seem to care much. Some well-aimed publicity might help us."

"It sure can't hurt," Eric interjected.

"Why don't you two give it more thought, and maybe I can interview you for the paper or on the air. I've got to figure out what would work best," Karen said, then waved at Brian. Karen's boyfriend, Dee, and Marc were installed in the bleachers, downing their lunches. Promising to catch up with Eric and Katie early the next week, Karen hurried off to join her friends.

Katie sat behind the backstop peeling slivers of green paint off a bench with the tip of her fingers. On the other side of the fence, men from the Rose Hill Bar and Grill softball team were taking batting practice. Now and then a ball banged against the chain link fence, jarring Katie's back, but she hardly noticed. She was sitting shoulder to shoulder with Eric. It had taken them most of the afternoon to find some time alone together. Now that they had finally escaped the rest of the gang, Katie suddenly found it absurdly difficult to talk to Eric. Especially with his shoulder pressed against hers like this.

She gave him a sidelong glance. He was staring very intently at his plate full of food: three hot dogs, a mountain of potato chips, two pickles, coleslaw, and a soda. All she had learned about Eric in the past ten minutes was that, thin as he was, he ate a ton. And being next to a girl he seemed to like had absolutely no effect on his appetite. In spite of her active life, a gymnast like Katie had been trained since childhood to watch her weight. Not that watching her weight was a problem just then. Someone could have set a Sticky Fingers Super Fudge Sundae in front of her, and she couldn't have swallowed a spoonful. Not with Eric so close.

She realized she was staring at him, so she shifted her gaze across the grass. The sun was bright in the western sky, and she closed her eyes and tilted her face back, drinking in the warmth.

Eric's smooth easy voice startled her. "So tell me something about yourself," he said. Her eyes popped open. She looked over at him. His plate of food was gone. For a second she thought she had fallen asleep, then she realized he had put it aside. Maybe he wasn't as hungry as he thought he was, either. That thought pleased her. Maybe talking to her alone like this frightened him a little, too.

"Ohhh." She bit her lip and smiled. "I don't know." She shrugged. "What kind of thing?" She traced a pattern in the dirt and wriggled her toes inside her pink hightops.

One side of Eric's face dimpled when he smiled. "What's your favorite thing?" he asked.

"Winning!" Katie answered instantly. "Winning in front of a big crowd. Like last week at St. Mary's Prep. Hardly anyone I knew was there, but the people cheered anyway when I came off the balance beam." She thumped the ground to show how solidly she had landed. Her eyes glowed with the memory. What a feeling!

Eric laughed and slapped his hand against his thigh. "Me, too. I like winning. Though in the pool you don't hear the crowd very much."

Katie looked at him hesitantly. "Earplugs!" he explained.

Eric's earplugs suddenly struck Katie as very funny. She began giggling, then he was laughing along with her, too. They were holding each other's arms, giggling uncontrollably, until tears streamed down their cheeks. Katie tentatively wiped her face and realized her lips were only inches from Eric's. She caught her breath. So did he. Then suddenly he began talking very fast, and Katie inched away slightly, struggling to breathe normally.

"You sound like you belong in the Olympics," he said brightly. "Loving the crowd and all."

"No, not at all," Katie answered. "I'm not good enough for the Olympics."

"That's not what I heard!" Eric exclaimed, looking directly at her again. His face registered genuine surprise.

Katie shook her head sadly. "I'm not. That's that. So many girls are into gymnastics, and so few have the right stuff. The competition's fierce, and besides," she said, "I'm too old now."

Eric's eyes widened. "What? Aren't you just sixteen or so?"

"Sixteen is over the hill for gymnasts on the Olympic level — only one or two girls have competed at that age. It's probably different for men's swimming."

Eric nodded and stared off into space. "Yeah.

I guess that's right." His broad forehead creased with a frown. He let out a sigh and looked back at Katie, considering her carefully. "For someone whose favorite thing is winning, you don't sound all that upset about not 'going for the gold'."

Katie smiled wistfully. "Don't get me wrong. I still dream about it. You know, the judges stand, the national anthem, me" — she mugged a heroic face — "doing a split on the front of a Wheaties box." Her voice was light and musical but her eyes grew serious. "But I don't just do gymnastics to win. I can't help myself. I love pushing my body that way, to its limits. I always have. I want to be first, but even if I come out last I love doing it. I love the competitions, the whole scene."

Eric looked at her with envy. "I don't feel like that," he said. "I *hate* losing." Abruptly he fell silent.

Katie wondered if she had said something wrong. She waited for him to continue, but he was staring down at his plate. He poked listlessly at his mound of coleslaw with a plastic fork. After a long pause, she said lightly, "So now we know one thing each about each other. We both like to win. You like to win more."

"You won just now," Eric said, gesturing behind him toward the baseball diamond.

"You let me!" Katie retorted.

Eric started denying it. But Katie interrupted him. "If I hadn't hit that homerun in the seventh, it might have been a tie game. Why did you let me do that?" she asked, immediately wishing she had kept her mouth shut. But she held her breath waiting to hear his answer. She didn't like the idea of a guy thinking she was the sort of a girl who needed a head start to win a race, or an easy pitch to hit the ball. But still, the idea that Eric let her hit a ball because he liked her — as much as she *didn't* like it — flattered her.

Eric answered very truthfully. "I didn't know you were good at baseball. I wasn't pitching your first couple of times at bat. In fact, I wasn't even there — I was late for the game. I guess I didn't want to strike you out," he finished in a low husky voice. He bent his head down toward hers.

Katie sat very still and didn't move. Some distant part of her mind was saying the words over and over in her head. He's going to kiss you. Eric Shriver's going to give you your very first kiss. As if drawn by a magnet she felt her face move toward his.

"KAYCEEEEEEEEE!" a boy's voice rang out from over by the parking lot.

Katie and Eric sprang apart before their lips had even touched. Katie bounded to her feet, her face scarlet. "Drat!" she cried. "My brothers. There's a family reunion tonight, and my mother's here to get me." She wrinkled her nose. "Uh, I have to go," she said, grabbing her bat and glove.

"Hey," Eric said, so tenderly, Katie felt her knees buckle. He reached for her hand and pulled her back toward him. "Tomorrow — are you busy?" he asked.

She looked up at him. There was a smile on his face. She was sure he was going to try to kiss her again. But any minute now nine-year-old Danny would turn up, or Will — he was worse. He was fourteen and just beginning to get interested in girls. She'd never live it down if Will saw her kissing some guy behind the backstop. She took a couple of steps back from Eric, putting a discreet distance between them. She held on to her bat with both hands. Eric kept smiling at her, with that crooked, warm smile.

"Uh, no — " she finally replied, digging the toe of her sneaker in the dirt. "I'm not busy."

"How about that skating lesson? Up in Rosemont Park?"

Katie's eyes searched Eric's. "Sure. I'd like that. I live up on Magnolia, two-twenty-five." She blurted out her address and turned away to run across the lawn toward her mother's red Voyager.

Eric cupped his hands and shouted after her. "What time?"

Katie skidded to a halt. "One. Is that okay? Around one?"

Eric nodded and Katie's heart soared.

"Who was that?" Danny asked, as she climbed into the back seat of her mother's van.

"Oh, just a guy. He's captain of the swim team. His name's Eric Shriver," Katie said as casually as she could, and then began talking about the game, saying Eric's name every chance she had. "Eric did this . . . Eric said that. . . ." Saying it made it all seem so real: She'd see him tomorrow, he liked her, he had almost kissed her now, and tomorrow he would. Katie kept her fingers crossed the whole way home.

Chapter
5

A stiff breeze started up, and Greg's new sailboat sped across the purply waters of Lost Lake. The afternoon had turned cold but the deserted lake, encircled by forested mountains, pale pink and dark green with spring blossoms and tall pines, was breathtakingly beautiful — and very romantic. But Chris didn't feel romantic at all. She sat shivering in the stern of the boat, her mouth set in a thin line of disapproval, feeling very cross. She'd only been sailing with Greg once before — last summer on Chesapeake Bay. She'd had a miserable time then and she was having a miserable time now. Maybe she shouldn't agree to go sailing with Greg again. Stiff breezes, cold water, and icy blue skies seemed to have a negative effect on their relationship.

The sails snapped loudly in the wind, and Greg had to raise his voice to make himself heard. He was standing at the helm talking to Jeremy Stone and Diana Einerson about his crew team. Greg shoved his Chesapeake cap back on his head and carefully outlined his plan to build a larger boys' team and then start a girls'.

Jeremy didn't seem to be listening. He was crouched at Greg's feet, videotaping his graceful maneuvers around the small craft. Jeremy focused the camera on Greg as he expertly tacked across Lost Lake.

Diana hung on to the side of the boat for dear life. She had never been sailing before, and she looked a bit seasick. There was a decidedly greenish tinge to her usually pink cheeks, and her blonde hair was wet from the spray and lay close to her head. The beautiful girl from Montana definitely looked out of her element and almost as miserable as Chris felt. With her free hand Diana bravely held Jeremy's camera bag out of the range of the frothy water splashing over the side of the boat.

Diana cast a sympathetic look in Chris's direction. Diana probably thought Chris was cold and sick, too. Chris was cold, but she never got seasick. Chris tried to smile back, but her lips felt too stiff and her whole face too tight, and not just from the cold, either. She was seething inside.

She had been looking forward to spending the day with Greg on the boat, and then joining Phoebe and some of the crowd at the Hall's nearby mountain cabin for a barbecue. The weather was perfect, if a bit chilly, and the two-hour ride up into the Western Maryland hill country had been fun, with Chris and Diana teaching the guys songs from summer camp they used to sing when they were kids. They arrived to find the lake nearly empty, and the mountain air clear. Everything had seemed perfect. She should have known it was too good to last. The minute Greg's new boat hit the water, Chris obligingly splashed ginger ale over its white bow and christened it the Sally Ride II, after her favorite heroine. Then Greg began talking about crew and that was all he had talked about all afternoon. Crew this, crew that, all his detailed plans for adding on to the boathouse, buying new shells, hiring more coaches, and dozens of other schemes for boosting the Kennedy team. Chris felt that she had just launched some kind of advertising campaign, instead of Greg's new boat. It seemed calculated to convince her to throw her weight around and be sure crew got more than its fair share of funds.

As they sailed up and down the mountain lake, Chris kept telling herself she was being unreasonable. Greg was just confident — he wasn't trying to sway her. But Chris wasn't convinced. She had gone over some preliminary figures that morning and at first glance, crew was way down on the list of who deserved funds according to the school board's new directives. Greg should realize that.

If Greg had been Ted or any other guy Chris had dated, she'd see his confidence was simply wishful thinking. But Greg was too smart about money. It meant only one thing — he must really believe deep down inside that Chris would find him funds simply because she loved him. The thought made Chris's stomach knot up.

"Can we go back now?" she finally shouted,

looking ruefully back over her shoulder. Jeremy's station wagon shone in the distance, the one metallic maroon dot in the otherwise empty Fillmore Nature Preserve parking lot.

"Oh, not yet!" Jeremy wailed. "Look at the light, it's so perfect." Greg either didn't hear Chris's protest, or else he purposely ignored it. Chris couldn't tell which. Sometimes it was hard to tell what he was feeling. But Greg had a sixth sense when it came to her moods. Chris knew he sensed she was miffed, and knowing that fueled her anger. She felt like prodding him, getting these funny suspicions out in the open. Instead, she pursed her lips tighter and focused her eyes on the water.

Jeremy's voice suddenly rang out across the sailboat. "Sound's like you've got it all sewn up — "

Chris's head whipped around. Jeremy was busy exchanging his camcorder for the 35 millimeter camera in the bag Diana was holding for him. But his shrewd eyes were on Greg, and he wore a very knowing expression on his face.

Greg cocked his head, and looking squarely into Jeremy's blue-gray eyes said, "What's sewn up?"

"The money. I heard that sports funding was going to be real tight next year. Especially for you little guys — " Jeremy paused to consider his pun. He looked up at all six-feet-two of Greg and started to grin. With a knowing glance toward Chris he continued, "Of course, mate, you've got an in, wouldn't you know."

"You don't have to remind him about that!

Greg's been conducting an all-out campaign to-day trying to win support from a certain quarter for his crew team," Chris suddenly cried. She jumped up from the narrow seat, rocking the boat in the process.

Diana gave a little shriek. Chris stood a second longer glaring at Greg, then plopped back down again, once more rocking the boat. She took a quick angry breath. "In fact, Greg," she said, tossing her blonde braid over her shoulder, "I don't know why you keep beating around the bush. Why don't you come right out and tell me, tell everyone — " she looked from a confused Jeremy to a startled Diana, back to Greg, "that you expect your crew team to win next year be-cause you expect to get more funding than any-one else in the school simply because you're my boyfriend. Why don't you just come right out and say it, instead of beating around the bush all after-noon."

Greg's mouth fell open. "Are you serious?" he gasped. His ruddy cheeks turned a bit pale, and his brow furrowed into a frown. "I don't expect anything from you, Chris! I can't believe you actually said that." He stared directly at Chris with a hurt expression. After a moment he abruptly turned away and fooled with the rudder. An embarrassed silence fell over the group and no one said a word until the small craft reached shore.

Phoebe Hall tiptoed out of the circle of firelight holding her Irish grandmother's thick woolen shawl over one arm. In her other hand she held a forked stick full of charred and drippy marshmallows still glowing from the coals of the barbecue pit.

"Chris?" she whispered, searching the dark shadows from the eaves of the cabin roof.

"Over here," Chris responded dully. Her voice was soft but to her own ears sounded harsh and shrill, like the sound of a fork scratching across a plate.

A sigh in the dark led Phoebe to Chris's side. She first poked the shawl in Chris's direction, then dropped down beside her on the patchy damp grass and offered her friend the first marshmallow.

Chris gratefully took the shawl. Cool twilight had given way to an almost cold mountain night. She pulled the wrap around her shoulders, on top of her sweat shirt, and with one fringed edge discretely wiped a tear from her cheek. With her other hand, she gently pushed the marshmallow away.

Phoebe's eyebrows shot up but she wisely didn't say anything. She popped the marshmallow into her own mouth and savored its charred, sticky sweetness. "Does this remind you of anything?" she asked casually, looking at the rest of the crowd huddled around the fire.

Chris swallowed hard. She started to say no, then followed Phoebe's glance. Holly Daniels and Bart Einerson were sitting with their backs propped against one another's very close to the fire. Holly's eyes were closed as she harmonized in a pleasant contralto voice with Bart's rendition of "Old Man River." Bart's guitar made a sad kind of sound, and the music drifted toward Chris.

A couple of months ago Holly and Bart had almost broken up. She had never heard the whole story — something to do with Bart's crazy flirting routine and Matt Jacobs falling in love with Holly. But the two of them looked so happy these days. Chris wondered what had made things work again. Suddenly how another couple fought and made up was of great interest to her.

"I'll tell you what it reminds me of." Phoebe's musical voice finally broke the silence and she answered her own question. "Camp. Remember Camp Cumberland the summer after eighth grade? What's the first thing you remember about that summer? Answer me quick." Phoebe ordered. "Don't think."

"Boys!" Chris said, and surprised herself by laughing.

"Not boys plural, Chris. One boy, remember?"

Chris cocked her head and tried to remember that summer. All of a sudden, it was hard to remember being thirteen and whatever it was that had made that summer so important. All she could think about now was tonight and Greg and how they hadn't exchanged a single word since their spat on the boat. The rest of the afternoon and all night long now, Greg had thrown himself into helping out Phoebe's dad rototilling the garden and starting the barbecue. He was still talking to Mr. Hall. Chris couldn't see Greg's face. He sat straddling the picnic bench with his back turned to her.

"I guess I just remember boys," Chris finally said with a sigh.

Phoebe tsk-tsked in the dark. "The counselor,

Chris. The tall, dark counselor from the University of Montana who was always playing guitar," Phoebe supplied.

Suddenly Chris remembered. She even remembered his name. "I know. Tom Perkins. You had such a crush on him."

"So did you," Phoebe reminded Chris, prodding her in the ribs with her elbow.

"That wasn't a crush," Chris said. "It was love."

"Want to talk about it?" Phoebe suddenly said.

"Tom Perkins?" Chris pretended not to understand.

"Chris," Phoebe warned. "It doesn't help to pretend nothing's going on. Besides, it's not like you. I mean, what are friends for? Don't tell me I'm getting obsolete."

Chris propped her chin on her knees and stared across the lawn into the fire. "We had a fight." She paused. "Greg and I."

Phoebe nodded and waited for Chris to go on.

"All day long he talked about crew, about what the team is going to do next year. He acted as if he didn't have the slightest doubt his team would get enough funds to continue — and grow." Chris abruptly turned around and faced Phoebe. "Pheeb, that's dumb. He knows crew's probably got the worst chance of any team to get more money. In fact, it's got the best chance to get less. And Greg's too smart not to realize that."

"But it's his team," Phoebe reminded her, a little puzzled about why Chris was so upset. "Of course he believes in it."

Chris drew back slightly and leaned her head against the side of the house. "So you don't think

58

it means he's trying to con me into fixing figures, or something like that? Into — " Chris hesitated before voicing the distasteful word, " — cheating because I love him?"

"Chris, you know Greg would never do that!" Phoebe cried, then clapped her hand over her mouth. No one else seemed to have heard. She lowered her voice and continued. "I'm sure that's the furthest thing from his mind."

Chris smiled. "Whew." She pushed the stray wisps of hair back from her temples and shook her head. "This whole thing has me so confused. I can't even think straight. Yesterday, Jonathan and Woody made jokes about Greg having an in with me. Now today Jeremy said — "

"Stop it, Chris," Phoebe interrupted. "Sometimes you just take things too seriously. Of course people — friends in particular — are going to kid you about stuff like that. Why not? But no one who knows you would *ever* think of you cheating." Phoebe tugged her thick red braid thoughtfully. "In fact, I'm more worried about Greg getting what's due to him," she said.

"What?" This time it was Chris's voice that rang out across the yard. Everyone looked over in their direction. She shrunk back slightly into the shadows. "What do you mean by that, Phoebe?" Chris demanded in a low, sharp whisper.

"I'm afraid you're going to bend over backward to prove you're fair. Swimming and gym and track are going to get the benefit of the doubt, so to speak." Phoebe shook her head and wished she had kept her mouth shut.

"Well," Chris said, and stood up and dusted off her crisp khaki pants, signaling her intention to end the conversation. "I can promise you one thing, Phoebe, no one, and I mean no one, is going to get cheated as long as I have anything to do with this funding crisis. I think the whole issue stinks. But since it's my job to do, I'm going to do a good one," she declared. "So far, I've never let my feelings interfere with any job I've had to do, and I'm not about to start letting them interfere now." She tilted her slightly pointed chin into the air and started gathering plates and cups off the table nearby.

"Come on, Chris. I'm sorry," Phoebe said and made a gesture with her hands for Chris to calm down. But Chris was already walking away toward the kitchen and didn't see or hear her.

Chris's blue Chevette was parked outside of Jeremy's house, just where she had left it that morning. She climbed in the driver's seat and unlocked the passenger door. Greg hesitated before getting in. He looked down the block, then thought better of attempting the three-mile walk to his house. It was well past midnight, the streets of Rose Hill were deserted, and he had already told Jeremy they'd take care of bringing the trailer and boat back to his place sometime the next day.

Still the prospect of going home in the car with Chris just then didn't exactly thrill him. Ever since that scene on the boat that afternoon Chris had been acting like some kind of ice princess, and Greg was hopping mad. He was also hurt and confused. He had no idea why Chris was suddenly on his case. Ever since yesterday's meeting she'd been pulling one weird trip after another. He was beginning to get sick of Chris's meaningful icy stares and defensive reactions every time he mentioned the words crew or boat. She was acting haughty, righteous, and very uptight. This was really the first major disagreement they'd ever had, and it didn't feel good.

In fact, Greg was aware of a hollow funny feeling in his gut. He pressed his lips together and focused his eyes out the window. He stared at the rapidly passing streetlamps without seeing them and forced back the awful empty sensation. He would be miserable if they broke up, and the thought of losing her made him sick.

Suddenly he noticed the car wasn't moving, and they were in the deserted parking lot on top of the overloop in Rosemont Park. The lights of Rose Hill twinkled below them. Off in the distance, the Washington Monument illuminated the starry night sky.

"Greg," Chris said.

He turned to face her, a confused look on his face.

She avoided his eyes as she said, "We have to talk." She clutched the steering wheel tightly and looked at her knuckles. "I'm sorry. About today. About blowing up at you. I made a mistake."

Greg let out a long, low whistle. He smoothed back his neatly combed hair and reached across the seat for her hand. Chris turned slowly toward him. Her blue eyes were soft with tears. "I kind of got the feeling back there, in the boat, that I had made some kind of mistake," Greg said as he stroked the palm of Chris's hand with his fingers. "I'm not exactly sure what you're mad at."

Chris's eyes held his for a moment. For a second Greg was afraid she didn't believe him. Then she nodded slowly. "I guess I wasn't very clear yesterday or today. I — " Chris searched for the right words. "I feel confused about being in charge of this funding, and being your girl friend."

Greg frowned slightly.

"I know I won't be affected by that. I won't play favorites. But I can't help worrying that other people feel I might — "

"Or should." Greg pulled his hand away and folded his arms across his chest. He toyed with the drawstring on the hood of his madras jacket. "You actually think I *expect* you to play favorites," he said as the realization sunk in. That's what's going on. You think I'd *use* you!" Greg's obvious shock at the idea was evident in his voice. He finally understood Chris's accusations on the boat.

Chris breathed a long sigh of relief and took hold of his hand again. "I know, I know. It's dumb of me," she said with an embarrassed laugh. "I just worry so much about what's right, about doing what's right and fair and. . . ." Her words trailed off, and she looked at Greg with such an incredibly loving expression on her face that his heart melted instantly. "I love you so much," she cried passionately. "I really do. I don't want anything to come between us, Greg. This whole thing has gotten me so upset, I've treated you badly. Oh, Greg, please — "

Greg didn't let her finish. He couldn't. He unclasped her seatbelt and drew her toward him, not taking his eyes from her face. With one hand he gently pulled the pink grosgrain ribbon from the bottom of her braid, then ran his fingers through it until her silky golden hair tumbled loose to her shoulders. And Chris, who a little while before had looked so remote, so cool, so unapproachable, suddenly looked all soft and huggable.

"Greg!" she cried. "It's so late." But she wrapped her arms around him willingly as he buried his face in her hair and covered the downy skin on the back of her neck with a million little kisses.

"Chris," he murmured, "nothing's going to come between us. Nothing," he repeated just before his lips found hers in the dark. Their kisses were long and sweet, but somehow Greg wasn't able to push back the frustrating thought that Chris didn't trust his motives.

Chapter
6

The next morning Katie woke up with a smile on her face and blinked at the light pouring through the bright green-and-white checked curtains onto her bed. The sunlight glinted harshly against the row of trophies lining the shelf just under the windowsill. Katie squinted and rolled over on her back to stare up at the ceiling. She had the pleasant sensation that she had just awakened from a beautiful, familiar dream, a dream she had had before but couldn't remember.

She folded her arms behind her head and gazed dreamily across the room. The wall over her desk was papered end-to-end with posters and photos of famous women athletes: Mary Lou Retton, Martina Navratilova, Chris Everett Lloyd, Tiffany Chin, Nadia Comaneci, Julianne Mc-Namara, Evelyn Ashford, Joan Benoit. Katie's mother had recently been on one of her major redecorating sprees. Katie had accepted the new, crisp curtains, the white walls, the bright green trim on the old-fashioned molding, even the beloved old easy chair that had come back from the store unrecognizable in green-and-white chintz. But she hadn't let her mother touch her postered wall.

Outside her window, familiar Sunday sounds rose up from the yard. She heard the loud rattle of a ball teetering on the edge of the garage door basketball hoop, then the thump of it dropping through onto the cement walkway. Danny and Will's voices joined her father's in the driveway below. It was a typical Sunday morning in April. And since everyone was already up and outside, it must be pretty late. Katie yawned luxuriously. It didn't matter — it was Sunday. She rolled over again and found herself nose-to-nose with the spiral-bound Georgetown University notebook she used as a journal. It was lying open on her pillow, with a ball point pen clipped to the page. Only then did Katie realize she had fallen asleep last night with her bedside light on while she was writing in her journal.

She reached up, flicked out the lamp, and spotted a tattered yellow sheet of paper poking out of her notebook. She unfolded it and rubbed the sleep from her eyes. As she read, a smile spread across her face.

Hill Street Blues	*Rosebuds*
Kim Barrie, 1b	Matt Jacobs, 2b
Molly Ramirez, 3b	Peter Lacey, c
Katie Crawford, ss	Marc Harrison, cf
Ted Mason, cf	Monica Ford, 1b
Brian Pierson, 2b	Brenda Austin, 3b
Karen Davis, lf	Dee Patterson, lf
Fiona Stone, rf	Sasha Jenkins, rf
Jonathan Preston, c	Elise Hammond, ss
Ben Forest, p	Eric Shriver, p

Katie read Eric's name and sat bolt upright in bed. She thought of the game and the way Eric had almost kissed her behind the backstop. Katie's hand flew to her face. Then her eyes flew back down to the journal page. She winced, then blushed reading the last couple of words she had written before falling asleep. "Geez!" she exclaimed, slamming the notebook shut and hiding the yellow sheet inside. She would die if her brothers snooped around her room and saw the romantic mush she had scrawled just before falling asleep. And then that lineup card. She had no idea how she had gotten Woody's boldly scrawled game notes. She only remembered finding it in her shirt pocket, deciding to keep it forever, and kissing it good-night last night. There was a smudge of pink lip gloss near Eric's name. Katie felt utterly embarrassed.

"Eric!" Saying his name aloud, she remembered their date. She whirled round and looked at the clock radio. It was almost noon. Only an hour before he'd be there. She sprang out of bed, tore off the black-and-orange Orioles jersey she used as a nightgown, grabbed her robe, and raced down the hall to the shower.

Twenty minutes later Katie was still in her underwear blowing dry her thick straight hair, and staring woefully at the heap of clothes she had pulled from her closet and bureau. She'd worn her best pants yesterday. Now they were dirty and torn. How could she go on her first real date wearing one of her brothers' old football jerseys, or her treasured threadbare baseball knickers, or even a nice but boring set of hot pink, gray, or blue sweats? She had tons of workout clothes. Every style of leotard, every shade of tights. Leg-warmers upon legwarmers poked out of her open drawers. She switched off the hair dryer, shook her head dismally, and decided then and there she hated her entire wardrobe.

Katie flopped down in her easy chair and fingered the new stirrup pants draped over the arm. She had bought them last week for dance class but hadn't worn them yet. She picked them up and shook them out. They were black, and went with anything, including her roller skates. Tugging them on, she studied the effect in the mirror. She wasn't used to wearing anything so revealing and tight outside of practice, but still, she was slim enough to look good in the shiny stretch fabric. After two quick spins in front of the mirror, she stopped frowning and grabbed a kelly-green-and-black football jersey off the bed. Most of the letters were peeled off and it had a tiny hole under the arm, but at least it was clean.

She pulled it over her head. It was long and baggy, but the green went well with her jade stud earrings. With a belt accentuating her tiny waist, a pair of matching socks, and her black hightops, she'd look okay. She pulled an elastic around her ponytail and tied it with a black ribbon.

Katie made a mental note to snare Molly for a shopping spree at the mall to get a couple of outfits to help her look more like a girl and less like an escapee from Little League. Then she rummaged through the bewildering assortment of mascara tubes, eyeliners, lip pencils, and makeup brushes poking out the top of her Ocean City trophy cup. Katie took a deep breath and tried to steady her hand as she put on her mascara. Finally, she drew a fine but effective dark line on the lower lids of her already striking brown eyes.

"Kayceee!" Danny cried from the bottom of the stairs. "Some guy's here for you."

Katie gulped, checked her reflection one more time, and hurried down the stairs. Halfway down she had to dash up again. She was so excited about seeing Eric, she had forgotten her skates.

"I wasn't kidding when I said I haven't done this since I was seven or eight," Eric said, pulling on one of his skates with one hand and hanging on to the door handle of his cream-colored Mustang with the other.

Katie struggled not to laugh. Eric was obviously a well-coordinated athlete, and his face was fixed in a tough sort of grin. Nevertheless, he looked scared to death, just like a six-year-old on his first pair of skates. She wondered where on earth he had dug up the scuffed black skates.

"Oh, you'll get the hang of it," Katie assured him, though she sounded more sure than she felt. At the moment she was too confused to feel sure about anything. Eric had been very polite when he picked her up at her house, and she was sure her parents had liked him. When she and Eric had marched off to the car and Eric had opened the door for her, she looked back and saw Danny snickering behind his hand. Katie had been tempted to run back and flatten her kid brother. But she had restrained herself and climbed gracefully into the car without another backward glance.

The whole way up the hilly backroads leading to picturesque Rosemont Park, Eric had kept up a smooth pleasant conversation. Again she got the unsettling feeling that Eric was used to first dates and girls.

Mainly he talked about the funding crisis. He had come up with some good publicity ideas to pass on to Karen if she really did bother to interview him. Katie got interested, and by the time they drove through the majestic wrought-iron gates to the park she had forgotten this was a date, and that maybe today he would really kiss her. Still, just glancing at his profile sent a funny shiver down her spine and made her palms sweat.

"I guess this is it," he said, pushing himself off from the car and across the paved lot. Instantly his legs shot out from under him.

"Watch it!" Katie cried, impulsively grabbing

his hand before he could go down completely. His fingers closed tightly around hers. She looked up at him quickly, but he wasn't looking at her. He wore a panicky look on his face and was staring at the vast stretch of parking lot lying ahead. Beyond the lot was the roughly paved surface of a sidewalk that curved around the perimeter of the hilltop garden.

Katie felt sorry for Eric, and with her free hand patted his arm. "Don't worry. I won't let you fall," she said, avoiding his eyes.

She patiently steered him to the path. The sidewalk, in spite of its cracks, was easier to skate on. They slowly traced a path beneath the blooming cherry trees, around the moss encrusted monuments, the gray stone fountain, and back again. They held hands the whole time, though by now Eric was skating more steadily.

"I'm getting it!" he cried jubilantly. "You're right. It's all coming back to me."

Katie grinned. "Good. Then it's time to take off the training wheels."

"Do what?" Eric asked, baffled. All at once Katie dropped his hands. Eric groaned and flayed his arms wildly.

He looked toward her helplessly, but Katie just smiled and shook her head back and forth. "Let's see how you do on your own now." She skated a little ahead of him and turned around. After a cautious check over her shoulder, she began skating backward, beckoning for him to skate toward her. "Take it slowly," she warned as they turned the corner beneath the archway of trees. Her warning came too late.

Eric had sped up just a little, trying to catch up with her. All at once he lost his balance, and his legs began going out from under him. He reached for Katie. She reached for him. Together they tumbled into a deep pile of cherry blossoms.

"Are you okay?" Katie asked, trying to catch her breath. Eric had landed on top of her and knocked the wind out of her.

Eric looked startled and reached down to rub his shins. "None the worse for wear!" he declared, then rolled over on his back and began to laugh uncontrollably. Katie sat up and massaged her elbows. They smarted where she'd hit the ground. Katie looked at Eric, chuckling merrily. His Cardinals letter jacket was covered with pink blossoms and some were caught in his hair. He looked sheepish and embarrassed and a little silly. But very, very handsome, too. "Do I look like you right now?" she asked, her eyes shining.

"What?" he gasped in mock horror. "You mean my hair's all red?" He sat up and gingerly patted his light hair. The blossoms showered down to his shoulder and onto Katie's arm. She squinted her eyes and pummeled him lightly on the chest.

"Don't you make fun of my hair," she reproached him, pretending to be offended. "It's not red — it's auburn." He grabbed her hands in his. Katie tried to pull away, but he was very strong and his hands around her wrists made her arms go soft and weak.

Eric's thick eyebrows arched up. "Sorry," he apologized, without letting go of her hands. The laughter died on his lips and he stared into her eyes. Katie sat very still, her legs sticking straight

71

out in front of her, and gazed right back into Eric's eyes. Everything seemed to stop: her heart, her thoughts, the sound of the birds chirping overhead, even the cool breeze. Katie thought for a moment the world had stopped turning. Still holding her wrists, but very lightly now, Eric leaned toward her. Katie closed her eyes just before he kissed her. His lips were gentle and sweet. He pulled back a little and took her face between his palms. She hesitantly put her small hand on the back of his neck and pulled him down to the ground toward her, and their lips met again in a deeper, more passionate kiss.

When they finally broke apart, they lay in the cushion of grass and blossoms for a long time. Eric stared dreamily into Katie's eyes, brushing aside her long, straight bangs and tracing the outline of her high, smooth forehead with his finger. Little thoughts slowly began to surface in Katie's mind. Not even in her wildest dreams had she imagined kissing would feel like this. She wanted, right away, to try kissing him again. She closed her eyes. She wanted to remember this moment forever. The fragrant cherry blossoms, the faint scent of new grass. But there was another scent that Katie had trouble placing. Then she realized that Eric smelled not of aftershave or cologne, but ever so slightly of chlorine. An incredible wave of tenderness washed over her at that thought. She opened her eyes and smiled at him. Shyly she reached out and wound her fingers gently through his hair. Eric stroked the back of her hand, sending shivers up her arm. After what seemed like forever, he said, "You know what I like best about you?"

Katie slowly shook her head no and held her breath. She suddenly felt embarrassed. She wasn't used to compliments about her looks or anything like that. Her friends generally said she was cute, and a sports columnist last year had called her "the feisty gymnast with those beautiful eyes." She had clipped the column and tucked it into her journal. But no boy had ever complimented her about anything but sports. She drew back slightly and took Eric's hands between hers. "My muscles?" she joked, keeping a straight face. She propped herself up on one elbow and displayed her biceps proudly.

Eric gave her upper arm an obligatory squeeze and looked very impressed. "Well, that's not what I had in mind. I didn't think gymnasts were into weight training."

"Oh, we've got our secrets." Katie tried to keep up her bantering tone, but Eric's very nearness, the warmth of his body near hers, was setting her heart racing. She was finding it hard to talk.

"Seriously — " Eric said, moving his face closer to hers. "It's your smile. You've got the greatest smile, K. C."

Before Katie had a chance to be embarrassed or protest, Eric kissed her again, so sweetly it took her breath away. "Eric," she murmured when they broke apart. "You know, I've never been kissed before. I didn't think it would feel like this."

Eric pulled away from her and considered her

carefully, his green eyes full of love. "Well, I never would have guessed, but as I'm sure your coach has told you, practice makes perfect."

As Katie wrapped her arms around him and pulled him closer, she couldn't have agreed more. And practicing seemed like a very agreeable way to spend the rest of the afternoon.

Katie made Eric park his Mustang in the cul-de-sac at the end of Magnolia. She'd walk the rest of the way home. She was afraid she'd feel self-conscious sitting in a car with him right outside her own front door. Her family's row house seemed too small, too full of brothers, too close to neighbors, and not private at all. Sitting face to face with Eric with her legs stretched across the front seat of the car, and her feet resting in his lap as she demolished the remains of her strawberry ice cream cone, had seemed a very private special moment. Katie didn't want the whole Crawford clan looking on.

"Do you want to go to the movies next week?" Eric suddenly broke the silence.

Katie started to say yes, then the smile faded from her face. "Next week?" She rolled her eyes and gave a nervous giggle. "You aren't going to believe this," she said, then instantly contradicted herself. "Actually, you're the one person who will. I've got a big meet coming up at Potomac High next Saturday. I'm scheduled for extra sessions at school, plus extra workouts down at the Fitness Center with my teacher."

Eric's face fell. "I had forgotten about all that," he admitted, downing the last of his cone and

74

looking sadly at Katie. "I really wanted to see you again, soon."

Katie reached over to him, and planted a kiss on his lips. It was short and sweet and tasted of ice cream, but left them both smiling.

"Hey, what about next Sunday? We could go skating again." Katie's eyes were laughing as she waved a finger under Eric's nose. "You could use more coaching on those skates." Suddenly Katie banged her fist on her head. "Sometimes I am so thick," she said, sitting back on her heels. "Why don't you come to my meet on Saturday? You could come on the team bus. I'd really love to have you there. It's the one big competition before the states, and I might have a chance of clinching first place."

Eric drew his breath in sharply. It was his turn to groan. "I can't," he said, sounding genuinely miserable. "Next Saturday the swim team's got a regional match in Virginia. We'll be gone overnight. I don't even know when we'll get back Sunday. That's why I thought it would be better to go out some night during the week."

He reached for Katie's hand. They sat there contemplating their predicament a moment, then Eric started laughing. "So what's the big deal? We can go out Sunday night. I'm sure we'll be back early enough so you and I can hit Mario's for pizza."

Katie nodded and smiled bravely. "Yeah — what's the big deal? I may never get to go to your matches, you may never get to come to mine. People have worse problems." She tried to joke, but she didn't feel like Eric's missing her meet

Saturday was very funny at all. The idea of him not cheering her on from the sidelines kind of hurt. Still, there'd be other meets before the season ended — maybe even the states. With that thought Katie's face brightened, and she took Eric's hand. "I guess Sunday's not so far away," she said finally.

"It just seems so long until then," Eric said, bending over to kiss her.

She climbed out of the car and watched from the corner until Eric disappeared in the distance. She waited a moment longer before starting home. She walked very slowly, savoring her solitude. Her hand strayed to her lips, her neck, her hair, all the spots where Eric had kissed her. Half a block from her house, she paused and spun lazily by one hand around the base of a streetlamp. "I'm falling in love," a voice inside her said over and over. Katie couldn't remember exactly when she'd ever felt quite this happy.

Not even last week when she won her last meet. No, nothing in the world had felt like this. Nothing this perfect.

Another voice inside Katie's head said: Not quite perfect. To make her completely happy, Eric would have to be there next Saturday to see her go out in the giant new gymnasium at Potomac High and secure her team a spot on the states. Yes, she would have liked to share that moment more than anything. Having the guy she loved by her side to share her victory was the only part of her most cherished dreams that hadn't quite come true.

Chapter
7

Monday afternoon, Eric made his way across the quad toward the corner where he knew Katie's friends usually hung out for lunch. He slicked back his hair, still wet from the pool, and approached the group gathered on and around the tree-shaded benches. He had had a great time playing ball with Ted Mason's crowd Saturday.

For the first time, he had gotten a taste of what it was like to belong to the most popular crowd at Kennedy High. Everyone had been friendly and nice and not at all snobby or stuck-up. He had felt right at home. Still, Eric knew from experience that kids tended to act more exclusive around school where they were visible, and Eric hated feeling excluded. He generally avoided cliques and groups and spent his time with a couple of good friends he'd known since first grade plus one or two guys from the swim team.

"Pull up a patch of grass and make yourself at home!" Ted patted the ground next to him and welcomed Eric with a smile.

Eric stood a moment, his hands stuffed in his pockets while he looked around. Marc and Dee were sharing the end of the bench. Molly was leaning against the dark branches of a willow, staring off into space while Pamela Green sketched her portrait. Peter Lacey was lying face up on a bench, soaking up the sun. A nearby portable radio emitted eerie sounds followed by Brian Pierson's voice commenting on today's weird selection for the music segment of *News/ Notes*. Eric's smile dimmed. Katie wasn't there. "Uh — where is everybody?" he asked.

Molly laughed wickedly. "*Katie's* taking a make-up test in the chem lab. She missed out on midterms during the gymnastics meet last week."

"Lucky for her!" A pretty, curly-haired girl said wryly, looking up from her chemistry text book. "By the way, I'm Holly Daniels. Who are you?" she asked Eric with a radiant smile.

Ted instantly introduced Holly and Bart to Eric. "Eric's our famous captain of the swim team."

Bart shoved back his cowboy hat and joshed in a good-natured Western drawl, "Oh, I thought you were Eric Shriver, the lovestruck losing pitcher I've heard so much about."

"What?" Eric recoiled from Bart's jibe sharply.

"Come off it, Shriver." Peter spoke up. "Plain as day you let Katie hit those runs Saturday."

"Believe me, I didn't let her hit that last run," Eric retorted, a rueful note in his voice.

Ted rolled his eyes. "I don't know how else she hit that last pitch," he said. Then, sensing Eric's wounded pride, he reached up and thumped him on the back. "Listen, letting a girl win now and then isn't so bad. Just don't make a habit of it."

Molly jumped up. "Come on, Ted. We know you're just jealous because Katie hit the same pitch that whizzed right by you out of the park."

"Molly," Pamela groaned, tossing aside her stick of charcoal. "You are the worst model. I give up."

Molly paid no attention to the soft-spoken artist and planted her hands on her shapely hips. "You know, Ted, all you guys — " She looked around giving Bart, Peter, Ted, and finally Eric each a long, hard stare. "Katie Crawford didn't need anyone to let her win the other day. In fact, if she weren't so into gymnastics, she'd probably join the Kennedy baseball team, and that would put all you guys to shame."

Eric felt the heat rise up his neck, clear to the top of his head. He was blushing red as a beet. "Don't look at me." He tapped his chest with his hands and shook his head vehemently. "I didn't say I let her hit that last homer Saturday. Because I didn't let her. She outsmarted me," he admitted grudgingly.

Bart punched Eric lightly in the arm. "Don't look so down about it. We're just teasing, you know."

Eric shrugged defensively. "Who looks down?" he asked, forcing a smile. "I'm just sorry I lost the game. I hate losing."

"So does Katie Crawford," Marc commented. "She's got quite a reputation for being one of the most competitive athletes on campus."

Ted agreed heartily. "In fact, my man," he said turning to Eric. "You're going to have quite a time keeping up with her."

"We'll see about that!" Eric warned with a smile. But Ted's comment stung just a little because Eric sensed it was true. From what he had heard about Katie's performances during gymnastic competitions, he knew before he'd ever laid eyes on her she was one of the top athletes in the school — male or female. And she had more than just natural talent. She had what his own coach called *heart*, that extra will to push, and the drive to succeed, no matter what. Of course, no matter how much determination you had, you still had to be super talented to win. Eric knew from watching Katie play softball she had that, too. Those two qualities combined had made her a local star.

While Eric was proud of Katie, deep down inside he felt uncomfortable with the thought that unlike Katie, he wasn't a star. He knew he was a good, all-around swimmer with a mean butterfly that wowed the judges, but he seldom ranked above second or third in the regional events. He was the best swimmer on Kennedy's team, but he certainly hadn't scored high enough to earn Kennedy a berth in the forthcoming states. He hadn't been able to singlehandedly pull his teammates through to victory like Katie had.

He shook his head trying to shake off that thought and forced his attention back to the football discussion Ted and Bart were having. Soon Karen Davis's voice replaced Brian's on the radio. She began editorializing about the plight of the underfunded sports, and Eric's nagging envy of Katie's competitive edge receded to the back of his mind.

Karen Davis pushed her red-rimmed glasses up on her nose and shielded her eyes from the sun. She gazed across the gently sloping lawn of Potomac Park toward the banks of the river. Suddenly she grabbed her friend Dee Patterson's arm.

"There he is. I see him." She pointed toward the newly erected Kennedy crew boathouse. Greg Montgomery towered over a group of guys who were painting the outside white. Another gang of kids clustered around a wooden shell that hung in two slings on the lawn. Karen pulled out her pen and notepad and briskly started down toward the river.

Loading her camera as she went, Dee struggled to keep up with her long-legged friend. "Do you think it's a good time to talk to him about the crisis? He looks so busy," Dee remarked as they neared the boathouse.

Karen nodded vehemently. "The best time. You'll be able to get some good high-interest shots to perk up the copy, and Greg will more or less have his guard down. That will make a better interview," she said with the practiced air of a seasoned reporter. True to her promise to Eric and Kate, Karen was determined to give the underdogs in this funding crisis a fair shake. Today's interview would be in Thursday's paper. She had already sparked interest in the plight of the underfunded sports with her noontime broadcast editorial. When she had turned up in the cafeteria for her own lunch period, the place was buzzing with sports talk.

She didn't know if she'd convinced anybody to support swimming or gymnastics or the other minor teams, but at least she had already managed to make the matter more controversial, to get the kids thinking about what they wanted to support in the long run. As far as Karen Davis was concerned, her job as a responsible newsperson was to present the facts and to let people come to their own decisions. Whether she agreed with those decisions or not was beside the point.

"So how do you like our setup?" Greg asked Karen a few minutes later. Dee was busy snapping photos of rowers and the volunteers from the Fix-It Club who were busy sanding and shellacking the shell. Matt Jacobs had obligingly climbed onto the roof of the small boat house and was pretending to drive in the last nail, though the roof had been completed last Friday.

Karen looked around the busy scene and smiled with approval. "I'd say you've got quite a setup here, Greg. Tell me, exactly how do you think any possible funding cuts will affect you and your team?" Again Karen studied the work crew. The kids were all covered in paint, and sweating in the warm spring sun, but every one of them appeared to be enthusiastic, happy, and pleased to be part of crew team's herculean effort to make something of itself. Karen had heard

Greg had a way of inspiring people to work hard and make impossible things happen. She had looked forward to interviewing him for just that reason. "The way you have your team working, Greg," she continued, "it looks like you think crew is going to not only survive this crisis, but thrive on it."

She stood with her pencil poised ready to jot down his response. Greg eyed his teammates proudly and twirled his cap on his index finger. "Well, you said it yourself. I'm determined to make it thrive. I have no reason to believe we won't get the funds we need." With a sly laugh he added, "Of course, not the funds we *want*, but we'll manage. I'm absolutely sure of that." His jaw was set and his clean-cut face looked stony with determination. "Besides," Greg added with a wink, "If things start to look bad, I've got a few strings I could pull."

Karen frowned before writing down what he had said. "You mean you don't expect to lose any funding?" she asked, not quite sure how to phrase her question. Something about his answer set off a warning bell in her head. Then she quickly remembered that she was supposed to be interviewing him and jotted down his first comments, word for word.

He waited for her to finish, then answered her second question. "Why should I expect to lose funding? That would be pretty self-defeating. There's always a way to make things work, to make dreams come true." Greg considered his own remarks then burst into a hearty laugh. "Gosh," he said, smoothing back his close-cropped hair, "I sound like the tooth fairy."

Dee, who was standing nearby, cracked up. Karen smiled. "I'll leave out that last part. I assume that was off the record," she joked.

Greg mopped his brow with an exaggerated gesture and bowed from the waist. "Thanks for that. I don't want anyone holding me responsible for quarters under their pillows." Greg looked over Karen's shoulder and anxiously surveyed his staff of painters. "Listen," he said evenly, "I've got a lot of work to do, unless there's more."

"No, no. I've got what I came for." Karen said, "Just let me read back what you said. I don't want to misquote you or anything."

Greg listened carefully and congratulated Karen on her accurate reporting. Then he waved a cheery good-bye and joined Matt and Cassandra Phillips over by the second boat where they were beginning to fiberglass a crack in the hull. Matt had the know-how, but Greg wanted to supervise the delicate business of making sure the seams were tight.

Gnawing the eraser end of her pencil, Karen studied Greg a minute before turning away and heading back across the quad.

After a long silence, she finally asked, "Dee, what do you think of Greg?"

Dee stopped in her tracks to ponder Karen's question. "He's a nice guy. I don't know him real well, but I like him. Uh, why do you ask?"

"Well. . . ." Karen hesitated. "I don't know. It's a hunch I guess. And sometimes my hunches are awfully wrong." She faced Dee, and her large dark eyes were very serious. "Greg sounded a little too sure of himself just now. Everyone else I talked to — Katie and Eric and Tara — they're all worried, mad, determined to fight to get what's due their teams." Karen paused and tapped her pencil against her chin. "Greg sounds like he doesn't have a worry in the world."

"That's just his style," Dee said promptly.

"I'm not so sure," Karen contradicted. "He's the kind of guy who can't bear the idea of losing out. He's a real entrepreneur. If Greg believes in something, he goes for it. Nothing gets in his way. And Dee — " Karen looked around and lowered her voice. "He's Chris's boyfriend."

"And everyone thinks that she's going to favor him," Dee said. "I heard the kids talking about it today over lunch. Woody and Jonathan were teasing her about it last week even. Chris got mad. But still, in her shoes. . . ." Dee shook her head in sympathy. "I don't know what I would do. I sure wouldn't want my boyfriend's team to suffer."

"But Chris has such impeccable ethics," Karen mused aloud.

"I know. And that's just what Elise said at lunch today. The way Chris is going to present the budget interests people a whole lot more than if any of the teams survive or go under because the school board's acting so stingy."

Karen was sure Elise was right. She knew mounting interest in the budget crisis had something to do with her WKND editorial, but it probably had more to do with Chris Austin and her reputation as one of the most fair-minded and honest people in the school and the fact that her boyfriend was the founder and captain of one of the teams most likely to suffer from cuts. Everyone would be watching Chris like a hawk.

Karen didn't know what to make of Greg's confidence. He sounded too sure of himself. Too cocky. Too convinced he had nothing in the world to worry about. Karen was almost positive Chris Austin would never play favorites on purpose, but how fair could a girl be when her boyfriend's dream was at stake? Her feelings had to get in the way. Karen tried to think how she'd act if she were in Chris's shoes and funding for Brian's music show was threatened. She'd try to make a fair decision, but wouldn't she be swayed just a little?

The whole way back to school, Dee chatted merrily about the boathouse, next month's prom, and a million other things Karen didn't pay much attention to. While Dee drove, Karen mulled over Chris's predicament. The issue didn't just involve being partial to Greg. It involved the problem of not playing favorites with any of her friends. As a student leader, Chris's best friends were naturally other student leaders — team captains, club presidents. At one time or another they'd all be involved in any funding decision Chris would have to make — no, Karen corrected herself, that *any* student body president would have to make. And that was a problem. Maybe it was unfair for the student body president to be in charge of funding matters like this. That was the real issue here, the one she needed to write about.

Chapter
8

It was Thursday morning. On her way to homeroom, Chris had picked up a copy of *The Red and the Gold* from one of the wire bins in the school lobby. She started reading as she walked through the crowded downstairs hall. She skimmed the article about a retirement party for one of the custodians coming up next week and turned to the second page. Her eyes lit up. Greg had mentioned Karen's interview would probably appear — with lots of pictures — in this week's issue. Chris slowed her pace as she neared the back stairs. She bit her lip and smiled gleefully. Greg looked absolutely great in the photo. She had to congratulate Dee Patterson next time she saw her. Dee's candid shots of the team and Greg were terrific. Chris started up the stairs as the first tardy bell rang. She hurried through Greg's interview and almost closed the paper when she spotted the headline of the editorial.

"Of all the nerve!" she practically shrieked out loud, giving the paper an angry shake.

THE REAL ISSUE:
FUNDING CRISIS OR CONFLICT OF INTEREST?

Chris's eyes narrowed. Slowly mounting the last couple of steps, she began to read Karen's editorial. With each word, a small crease in her forehead deepened. When she got to the end of the page, she really did shriek out loud, oblivious to the stares of other students as they milled around her on their way to class. The second and final bell rang. The hall emptied out, but Chris stayed rooted to the spot. She leaned back against the wall and reread each word of Karen's article. In short, it accused her of not being able to be impartial to her friends who were on teams most threatened by school budget cuts. Oh, it didn't mention any names, Chris noted grimly. Not one. But that didn't matter. Everyone would know exactly who she was talking about. Quite clearly and concisely Karen posed the very transparent question right there in black-and-white:

"How suitable is it for the student body president to be the one to decide the funding for her peers? Inevitably, one holding such a high elected office in the school can't be absolutely impartial to acquaintances and friends, who are sure to be among other student leaders, and who naturally will be on some of the teams involved. It's not fair to the student body president *or* to the teams concerned."

Chris was stunned. The editorial was well-written. She could almost hear Karen's voice reading it over WKND. Chris inhaled deeply and passed her hand over her burning forehead. She had never felt so angry in her whole life. The very thought that someone would actually accuse her so publicly of not being able to do her job felt like a punch in the stomach. Chris wouldn't stand for this. She'd find Karen now and clear this matter up. She'd demand an apology as loud and strong as the editorial.

Using her privileged position as president, Chris marched right past the hall monitor and she stomped around the corner to the newspaper office. Chris, Karen, and Sasha didn't have to turn up at homeroom regularly. On publication day, Karen often spent the morning working on her copy for her noontime broadcast.

Chris flung open the door and walked in without knocking. Karen looked up from the desk and met Chris's angry eyes without flinching.

Chris tossed the paper on the reporter's scrupulously neat desk, and tapped her foot angrily. "Do you want to explain this?" Chris said in a controlled, angry voice. Two little red spots burned in her cheeks, and her blue eyes flashed fire.

Karen exhaled and pushed her chair back. She got up slowly and pulled out a chair, motioning for Chris to sit down. Chris gave her a scornful look and chose to remain standing.

Karen perched on the edge of her desk, and poked her pencil into her ponytail. "I just wrote my opinion based on the facts, Chris. I'm sorry you got offended, but I have a job to do."

Chris stared hard at Karen. She didn't know her well, but she knew Sasha respected her reporter's integrity. Chris was surprised to see Karen look so cool, calm, and self-confident. Chris realized that Karen hadn't been out to get her with the editorial. She must have had some reasons for writing it, and Chris intended to find out what they were.

"I don't know what facts could possibly lead you to write that I am incapable of staying impartial about this funding crisis, or about anything else that has to do with my job. I would like you to retract that editorial immediately. Even though you don't mention any names, everyone knows exactly who — and what — you are talking about, Karen. *Everyone*," Chris repeated.

She eyed the chair Karen had pulled up, and after deliberating with herself another second, sat down. If Karen was willing to talk about this mess calmly, so was she. Chris folded her hands in her lap. She looked Karen directly in the eye and didn't even blink until Karen launched into her explanation of what had happened.

Chris was startled by Karen's first words: "Didn't you read the interview with Greg?"

Chris gave a little shrug as if to say, "so what." "I skimmed it," she admitted. "It's the editorial I'm here about. Not what Greg said to you or what you said to Greg."

"It all boils down to the same thing," Karen stated. She got up and paced over to the window. She jammed her hands into the roomy pockets of her pale linen pants, and after a moment, turned back toward Chris, her face troubled.

90

"After I talked to Greg, I came to the conclusion that you were going to favor him. Actually," she corrected herself quickly, "that he had reason to believe you were going to favor him."

Chris's mouth fell open. She reached for the interview, but before she could begin to read it, Karen continued. "I was wrong."

"What?"

"I was wrong," Karen repeated, as she marched up to Chris, her brow knotted with worry. "I made a mistake. I should have come to interview *you* first. Gotten your version of what's going on. But in any case, the interview with Greg just gave me the idea for the editorial. I don't know about retracting the piece because I believe in what I wrote, Chris. I really stand behind what I said there." She tapped her finger on the paper.

Chris fiddled with the tie on her wraparound skirt. "But it's just not true," she maintained.

"Then why don't you say that? Tell me why it's not true. But even if you can't convince me, you deserve the right to convince everyone else. Just go on WKND today during my air time and defend yourself, stating your case. That's fair. Isn't it?" Karen asked in a reasonable voice. "But read Greg's interview first. Please," she said and reached for Chris's arm.

Chris couldn't argue with Karen on that point. After all, her own discussions with Greg lately had left her with a funny feeling about this funding crisis. She calmed herself and began to read the interview. Very carefully, she read each question Karen had posed to Greg and each of Greg's answers. By the end she was seething. Not because of Karen, but because of Greg. No wonder Karen had thought Chris was playing favorites! Greg made it sound like she had the whole funding problem solved already, with one person coming out on top — Greg Montgomery. In spite of all his protests Saturday night, he had no intention of *not* using her. That was clear to Chris now.

Chris choked back her feelings of hurt and rage against Greg. With difficulty, she managed to keep her voice controlled as she stated her case to Karen. Karen listened intently and was convinced Chris had every intention of playing fair.

Before her news show on WKND, Karen explained that she still felt funding matters should be decided by the budget committee of the school board and the PTA, but she now had absolute confidence that Chris Austin would play fair. Then she turned the mike over to Chris.

Chris took a deep breath and blocked out the distracting dials and buttons on the control board of the WKND booth. She hated talking on the radio to the student body. It felt so impersonal, not being able to single out faces she knew in the audience and make eye contact. But she knew her honor was on the line, and that helped. "I know you'd rather hear Brian's new music show, rather than the same old voice of Chris Austin," she started lightly, "so I'll get right to the point. I'm sure everyone read Karen's fine editorial in today's paper. I don't know if she is right or wrong about who should or shouldn't be responsible for appropriating funds to the various sports teams. It's an interesting question that everyone should think about, discuss, and bring up at the next open school board meeting. But I just wanted to set everyone's mind at rest once and for all." Chris spoke her next words in a slow, deliberate voice. "I will not, under any circumstances, play favorites in this current budget crisis. I have never let my personal feelings interfere with my job here at Kennedy. I trust you to believe that that's why you voted for me last year. I promised to be fair, impartial, and a good student leader. Sometimes — " Chris's voice faltered a bit, but she came back quickly. "Sometimes I've been too quick, or outspoken. But I've never cheated anyone, and I never will." Her voice rang out clear and strong with her last couple of words. When Karen took over the mike, Chris turned away and quickly edged her way out of the tiny broadcast booth. She hid for a moment behind the sound-proof door. Monica, Peter, and Brian were gathered in the WKND office. Phoebe and Diana were out in the hall, standing by for moral support. She didn't want to face any of them just yet.

Chris dabbed her face with the sleeve of her pink cardigan. A single tear had started down her cheek. She was grateful to Karen for giving her a chance to clear the air and her name; Chris sensed her little speech would go over well. She knew that the kids respected and listened to anyone who was honest and sincere. They'd give her the chance she deserved to prove herself.

But the one person who really mattered most to her had let her down. And Chris wasn't sure she knew how to face him now or how to tell him how angry she was. How to say she wasn't sure she wanted to see him for a while.

Chapter
9

"That's it! That's the game!" Greg whooped with glee, though his triumphant smile looked a bit forced as he approached the net and vaulted over to Chris's side of the court.

Ignoring him completely, Chris untied her sweater from the fence enclosing Kennedy's tennis courts and started for the locker room.

In a couple of long strides, Greg caught up to her. "Aren't congratulations in order?" he asked in a hesitant voice. Chris had turned up late for their regular Thursday afternoon match and hadn't looked him in the eye once. She had played a fierce but overemotional game, losing to him hands down. Chris always lost to Greg. She was used to it. Greg waited for Chris to say something, but she just kept walking, her back stiff as a board.

He cleared his throat noisily, then he threw his hands up in the air and shouted after Chris,

"Okay, I give up. I think I'm beginning to get the *point*." He walked to her side but stayed just far enough away so they weren't touching. "I'm supposed to know why you're going through your ice princess routine," he said. There was a sharp edge to his usually even voice. "Come on, Chris. This isn't fair. I can't say I'm sorry. I can't even defend myself, unless you tell me what's wrong." Chris kept walking. Greg decided not to follow. If Chris wanted to give him the cold shoulder, he wasn't going to run after her. He had thought they'd cleared things up the other night. Now, here they were, starting all over again. Whatever was going on between them, he was getting sick of it.

Just when he was about to give up, Chris turned around. It was the first time she had looked at him directly all day. Her eyes were like steel. Inadvertently, Greg took a couple of steps backward.

Chris marched over toward him and said in a low voice, "I can't believe you don't know what's wrong. Didn't you read the paper today?"

Greg gaped at her. "You're upset about that interview?" He sounded so innocent and amazed.

Chris couldn't believe it. She tucked her racket under her arm and ran her hand down the length of her long blonde braid. "Greg," she said, forcing herself to keep her voice even. "I read that interview, and yes, I'm upset about it. So was Karen Davis. You've given everyone the impression that I'm playing favorites. You know you made it sound like that. Don't try to deny it," she added hastily before he had a chance to interrupt. "Because the evidence is in the paper in black-and-white. What do you think prompted Karen's editorial? W-What right — " Chris began to stammer, her voice trembling with anger. "What right do you have to presume crew is going to be just fine? 'I've no reason at all to believe crew won't get the funds they need.' Isn't that what you said, Greg? Isn't it?" Chris challenged him to deny it.

"Oh, this is too much," Greg said, and hurled his racquet across the grass. It rebounded against the base of a sapling cherry, nicking the tender trunk. Greg muttered a curse, then stomped off to retrieve it. He stomped back again, his teeth clenched, and stared squarely at Chris. "You — you and Karen and whoever else — keep twisting my words around. Sure I said that, something like that. Why should I think differently? I think we deserve funds, I think when the figures are down for everyone to see, that will be perfectly obvious. I'm not worried. Or, at least, I wasn't until now," he said, his eyes suddenly narrowing. "But I'm beginning to think you have no intention of playing fair, Chris. You seem to be determined to let me know, one way or another, that my team is *not* going to get what it deserves."

Chris threw her head back and groaned. "Now you sound like Phoebe. I am not going to give you, or crew, or anyone else more or less than what they deserve. Don't you understand?" she nearly screeched. Then what she hoped wouldn't happen did: She burst into tears. "I don't understand this. I don't understand what's happening," she wept, turning her back on Greg, her body shaking with sobs. Her head was pounding, her heart felt like lead, and what had seemed perfectly clear a little while earlier wasn't very clear at all. Greg didn't seem like the bad guy anymore, but she didn't quite believe he was the good guy, either. Suddenly nothing was making sense.

Greg's face softened. "Oh, Chris," he said, putting his hands on her shoulders. Her whole body tightened at first, then Chris couldn't fight her feelings any more. She loved Greg too much. Her shoulders relaxed, and she allowed Greg to turn her around and draw her toward him.

"Chris," he pleaded. "Listen to me. I just want a fair shake. No more, no less, than anyone else. I'm sorry if whatever I say seems to come out wrong. I just believe in my team. You can't blame me for that," Greg explained, as he stroked Chris's hair. Chris pressed her cheek against the smooth knit fabric of his shirt. She could feel his heart pounding though he sounded very reasonable as he said, "You're not the only one who believes in fair play, you know," he reminded her gently.

Chris swallowed hard and pushed herself away from Greg. She took the tissue he produced from his back pocket and blew her nose. Finally she looked at him. "I want to believe you, Greg," she said haltingly. "I really do." She sank down on a nearby bench and rolled her racquet between her hands. "Maybe I'm overreacting." She pushed a strand of hair back off her throbbing temples.

Greg surprised her by stating simply, "It's hard to ignore what people are saying."

Chris cocked her head and a small smile worked its way around the corners of her mouth.

"You never admitted that before. You're always telling me I shouldn't care about what other people think or say."

"You shouldn't care, but that doesn't make it any easier to ignore," Greg said. He offered her his hand and pulled her to her feet.

Chris looped her arm around Greg's waist and hooked her thumb in the pocket of his white shorts. Greg massaged her shoulder as they walked. Halfway back to the main building, Chris felt a sudden sense of relief. They weren't going to lose each other after all. All day long everything had seemed so hopeless, so difficult. Now, just talking out their problems had made everything better. She would try to trust Greg from now on. She owed him that much. After all, what had he ever done to make her distrust him so much? Love his team? His devotion to what he believed in was part of the reason she loved him.

"So," Greg said as they headed up the short flight of steps back into the building. "Have you made any decisions yet?"

Chris's head whipped around. She dropped her hand from Greg's waist and gave him an uncomprehending look. "Did you really just ask me that?"

Greg's easy smile froze on his lips. "What did I say this time?" His voice rose slightly.

"Nothing," Chris fumed. "Absolutely nothing." She pushed open the heavy metal fire door. Molly Ramirez's voice rang out from the gym. She was holding her Thursday afternoon self-defense session for the underclassmen. Chris could hear her shouting out instructions for some drill.

She took a deep breath and said to Greg through clenched teeth, "Greg, can we get one thing straight? I'm sick of talking about crew, about funding, about money. I have a lot of decisions to make in the next few days. I don't need your input. Besides it would be wrong to let you know what I have decided before anyone else. You'll hear the news next week at assembly, the same time as the rest of the school and not a minute before. Meanwhile, I don't want to hear another word about this. Okay?"

"Yes, *SIR!*" Greg shouted back and mocked Chris with a click of his heels and a smart salute. "It's always good to know exactly what's off limits," he added sarcastically. "And from what I gather, our relationship is off limits until Monday. Have a nice weekend!" With that, he turned and vanished into the boys' locker room.

"Greg?" Chris started to call after him, then thought better of it. She slowly headed down the long hall toward the girls' showers, trying to figure out exactly what had happened. She couldn't believe he actually meant that about the weekend. Chris felt like running after him, but she couldn't. It wasn't just her pride holding her back. This weekend she did have to make some pretty big decisions. Having Greg around would just make everything harder. Yet not having Greg around —

Chris touched her cheek and looked down the hall where Greg had disappeared. All day now, Greg hadn't kissed her. Now she wouldn't see him all weekend. Her arms suddenly felt empty, her stomach hollow. Knowing she wouldn't see him felt terribly weird. Chris drew her hand across her forehead and leaned back against the cool concrete wall. She fought back a panicky tide of fear. Was she losing Greg? She clamped her eyes shut and turned off that thought. Chris refused to let herself contemplate a future without Greg. Slowly the churning inside her subsided.

Somehow the funding crisis had turned into a personal crisis for her and Greg, and Chris had no idea what to do about it. She only knew she couldn't take these roller-coaster feelings: one minute furious, next minute crying, next minute loving, now angry again. The months of smooth sailing she'd had with Greg seemed to have finally hit a stormy patch. Chris was beginning to wonder if she and Greg could weather it.

If only she could talk to Phoebe or Brenda right now, and ask them to help her understand why everything seemed to be falling apart. But she couldn't. She couldn't risk being influenced about Greg or crew or anything. . . . Not until this weekend was over and she had made her decision about who got what money. She had to make that decision alone. The responsibility for presenting the unbiased facts and figures to the school board was solely hers. Input from her friends about her personal crisis with Greg might sway her one way or another. Somehow everything she felt about Greg, loving him, wanting him not to be hurt, had gotten all tangled up with the dumb budget cuts. Determined as she was to try, Chris didn't know how she'd manage to keep her job and her feelings separate.

Chapter
10

Katie lay with her chest pressed against the thick carpeted basement floor, and her legs spread out at a one-hundred-eighty-degree angle. She pillowed her cheek on the rug, closed her eyes, and taking one deep breath after another, let the stubborn knot she'd been feeling for days at the base of her spine stretch out. A burst of laughter from the living room upstairs filtered through the closed door. Danny and Scott and her mom were watching TV. For five weeks in a row, Katie hadn't been able to watch her favorite programs. She hadn't even had time to replay the tapes Danny had made for her. It was the height of the local gymnastics season, and Katie had to spend all her time working out: with the team, with her coach, by herself every night in what she loved to call the Crawford Workout Center.

Katie's brothers had some used weight-lifting equipment that her dad had picked up from a health club that was going out of business. But the boys no longer used it, so Katie had made her own private workout area in a corner of the basement. Besides the barbells, bench press, rowing machine, and exercise bike, the room was cluttered with a pool table, a pinball machine, and an antique jukebox that Katie sometimes used to play music to dance to and loosen up with before her weight-training.

Slowly she rolled up to a sitting position. She'd been stretching long enough. She shook out her shoulders and stood up. Just as she mentally began to review her workout, the phone rang. A goofy smile lit up Katie's face, and she looked hopefully up the stairs. But no one called her name. She glanced at the clock over the sagging old sofa. It wasn't time for Eric to call yet. He usually waited until after nine, until she was back from the gym, or finished with her private work-out.

She tightened the elastic in her ponytail and tugged down the back of her leotard. Every single night since Sunday, Eric had called. Just to hear her voice. Katie knew that was why he called. It was the same reason she loved talking to him, though nothing very new had happened to either of them all week long. Katie had been surprised how much she had missed him since Sunday. They'd only run into each other once since then — yesterday between classes at school.

Remembering how Eric had waylaid her outside of the language lab, Katie giggled. She wrapped her arms around herself and tried to contain the light, fizzy sensation she got whenever she thought about him. Since Sunday she had felt light as a balloon, barely touching the ground when she walked. Katie gave her head a shake and commanded herself to stop thinking about Eric. Fizzy feelings were all well and good, but bad for her balance, as Mr. Romanski had noted last night when she sprang through a tumbling routine and practically forgot to land. Katie decided to start with some sit-ups to get her mind off of Eric. Soon, however, her thoughts slipped back to gymnastics.

Katie loved the beam. She had the right flexible build for it: graceful and leggy, though she was short; a surprisingly good sense of balance; and the kind of dogged patience that made the beam her best event. Before her older brother Kevin had gone to college, he used to work with her in the gym as her spotter, easing her through new, difficult moves, time after time, breaking her inevitable tumbles off the four-inch-wide-beam. Now some of her handsprings and backflips seemed almost as natural as walking or breathing.

Of course, some moves never felt natural no matter how often you did them, Katie reminded herself as she finished her last sit-up. She pulled her bangs over her blue terry sweatband, exhaled deeply, and went over to lay down on the bench press.

She was trying to do reps with ninety pounds to increase her upper body strength. Katie took a deep breath, gripped her hands around the bar, and pressed it up over her head. But on the fourth press, Katie felt herself weaken — the bar was too heavy. When she brought the barbell back down, it slammed into its stand.

"*Drat!*" she cursed, massaging her strained arm muscles.

"You okay?" a concerned voice asked from halfway down the stairs.

Katie looked up. In a second she was on her feet, across the floor and in Eric's outstretched arms.

"What are you doing here?" She leaned back in his embrace and smiled delightedly up at him. His hands felt warm and reassuring on her back. Then Katie remembered she was wearing a very skimpy French-cut leotard and no tights. She colored slightly and extracted herself from Eric's arms. She reached for her terry cloth beach cover-up and slipped it on, tying the wide belt tight around her tiny waist.

"I got lonely," Eric said, leading Katie by the hand over to the sofa. She snuggled up against him and rested her cheek on his shoulder.

"Me, too," she admitted, then admonished him playfully. "But I didn't finish my workout yet. Remember, practice makes perfect." She sounded just like him when she said that — the way he had sounded Sunday when he kissed her in the park.

"Be my guest." Eric gestured magnanimously toward the weights.

Katie started to get up but Eric pulled her back down by his side, and taking her flushed cheeks between his hands, he drew her face toward him for a kiss. He kissed her neck, her face, her lips, and finally the tip of her ear. "Hmmm, feels like you've been practicing." He laughed huskily, his hands massaging her well-developed shoulders.

"Oh, I've always been a quick study," she quipped, a bit breathlessly, and tucked her legs under her on the couch. "So, what's new?" she asked, though she didn't really feel like talking. Eric looked kind of dreamy and confused and a faraway smile played at his lips. Katie figured she looked more or less the same way. Right then she just wanted to hold him and not say anything.

"Did you read this yet?" He tapped a folded copy of *The Red and the Gold* that was lying on the couch next to Katie's green canvas carryall.

Katie shook her head.

"Karen Davis is sure keeping her promise. Talk about publicity." Eric gave an appreciative whistle and opened to Greg's interview. Katie leaned forward and studied the pictures intently. "Wow, these are great shots!" she exclaimed. "I wish they'd come and cover the gymnastics squad — and the swim team," she added hastily. Something inside her didn't like the idea that though they were united in the effort to get funding for all the underfunded sports, they were at the same time rivals. It was team vs. team vying for the same portion of the economic pie. Katie reached for her sweat pants and socks, and pulled on her clothes, then read Greg's interview. The delighted expression on her face gave way to an annoyed look.

"The way this sounds, Greg's way off and running in the funding department," she commented.

"Exactly." Eric jumped up and walked over to the pool table. He racked up the balls and looked around for the cue. When he didn't find one, he hoisted himself on the table, and drummed his fingers against the shiny wood rim. "The interview is great. It got everyone all worked up over the funding crisis, except for all the wrong reasons," Eric lamented.

"Because he sounds so sure of himself?" Katie wondered out loud.

"No. Because he's Chris's boyfriend. It seems like he's counting on her to pull strings for him. At lunch today, everyone was talking about it. Chris got on the air to respond to Karen's editorial, and she swore she'd play fair and square. Lots of kids believed her, but some didn't. I don't."

"Chris? Pull strings? What are you talking about?" Katie exclaimed. She reached for the paper again and read Karen's editorial. Her response was immediate. "No way. Chris Austin would never do something unfair. I mean, Karen's right about who gets to choose who gets what — it's a tough job and a student shouldn't be in that situation. But Chris would never play favorites."

Eric got down from the table and paced the floor in front of Katie, who was sitting on the seat of her rowing machine, pulling a sweat shirt over her head. She had untied her ponytail to comb her hair. "Why wouldn't she?" he asked. "Think about it — Greg's the guy she loves. It must be hard finding yourself in the opposite camp from someone you feel so strongly about."

"No way! Romance shouldn't get in the way

of fair play, ever. If I were in Chris's shoes, if I had the slightest doubt I could be impartial, I'd quit," Katie said adamantly. She slid the rowing machine seat back and forth as she talked, and her face was flushed with excitement.

Before Eric could say another word, Katie hopped off the rowing machine and grabbed her bag. She pulled out a large green plastic brush and leaned forward, her straight red hair falling like a curtain in front of her face. As she brushed it with determined, strong strokes, she peered up at Eric, and said, "Like the other day. I mean, I like you, you like me, but it would have been wrong to miss that last pitch you threw just so you could win the game. My team needed me to win, and I had to do my best to come through for them. I might have missed the pitch or struck out. But I never would have done it on purpose."

A cautious expression stole over Eric's face. "Who said you would?"

Katie bounced up and tossed her hair back. "No one. No one said I would," she replied frankly. "But it's the principle of the thing. Don't you see? Chris favoring Greg is like me letting you win a game — or you letting me win, for that matter. Romance shouldn't get in the way of stuff like that."

"I don't think it's the same thing at all," Eric maintained. "Besides, it wouldn't be such a crime."

"How can you say that!" Katie cried, shocked. "If Chris favors Greg, then everyone loses out. You, me, Tara. Everyone but Greg. That's not right."

"I didn't mean that," Eric said grumpily, clenching and unclenching his fists. He strode over to the jukebox and randomly pushed some buttons. He was startled when lights started flashing and the current Number One song came on.

"You don't have to put a quarter in," Katie explained, studying Eric's profile. He looked so upset. She couldn't quite understand it. How could someone as into sports as Eric was not understand how important it was to play fair? Especially when not playing fair on Chris's part would threaten the very existence of his team.

As if reading her thoughts, Eric turned around and faced her. He threw his hands up in the air and said a bit sheepishly, "Gosh, we sound like we're fighting on opposite sides all of a sudden." He didn't sound very sure of himself. "The point is, that Chris explained herself on the radio. She said nothing personal would get in the way of her decisions, and I guess we just have to hope she was telling the truth. . . ." Eric's voice trailed off, and Katie sensed he was expecting her to say something, to let him know they weren't really having a disagreement or argument.

Katie didn't answer right away. She wasn't quite sure of what to say. She didn't want to argue with Eric, but she couldn't pretend to agree with him, either. She held her hair back from her face with one hand and toyed with the rubber band in the other. She looked down at the thick, dingy orange carpet and wondered what Eric was *really* upset about. She flashed on the game Saturday. When she had mentioned the game, that was when he had turned all weird. Katie wondered if he actually had expected her to have missed that last pitch because she liked him. If the situation were to come up again, did he expect her to try to lose, to not compete all out with him, and not give her all to win?

Katie didn't want to believe that. She wished with all her heart that she knew a bit more about boys. She felt like she was in the middle of a new, intense game, and she didn't know the rules. Everything seemed to change when a guy was more than just a friend. First chance Katie got she would ask Molly. Molly had lots of experience with guys and relationships. Besides, maybe Ted had said something to Molly about how Eric really felt about the game Saturday, if somehow inside he resented Katie for knocking in the winning run.

Eric cleared his throat, and the sound brought Katie back to the present. She realized she still hadn't answered his unspoken question. "Yes," she said, forcing a smile. "I suppose you're right, about Chris I mean. Knowing Chris, she probably won't play favorites. It's — it's just not like her," Katie concluded with conviction.

Chapter
11

Elise Hammond knelt on her seat and pressed her nose against the school bus window. She stared out into the rain at the hilly gray landscape. "I can't believe I've never been up this way before. Potomac is really beautiful," the curly-haired junior announced cheerily to Diana and Katie, then grabbed the back of her seat for balance as the bus circled down the exit ramp of the Interstate.

"Ever the optimist." Diana groaned and whopped Elise on the head with a copy of the western novel she was reading.

"Ouch!" Elise shielded her head and pretended to be mortally wounded. "Told you reading stuff like that would encourage latent, violent, cowgirl tendencies." Elise winked broadly at Katie.

Katie managed a wan smile and resumed her own vigil, staring out the window at the swiftly passing trees. Their trunks were very black and shiny from the rain. The meadows were in full spring bloom. Katie usually loved days like this. The air was fresh and damp, and the earth smelled alive and vibrant. But today she barely noticed. She knew there would be another half hour of winding back roads before the bus reached Potomac High, and it already seemed like they'd been on the road forever. Usually she took advantage of the long trip before a meet to unwind a little. She'd be so full of nervous energy she'd gab endlessly to whoever was nearby. But today she didn't have much to say. Not that she didn't appreciate the company of Elise and Di.

They were trying so hard to cheer her up. Today's competition was a big one. If she and her team placed first, they'd go to the states. If not, they probably wouldn't. Katie couldn't afford to be gloomy when winning was so important. Having an upbeat, positive attitude before a meet was always half the battle.

She tucked her hands into the warmth of her overall pockets and slumped down a little in her seat. Of course she was feeling a bit down-in-the-mouth, she reasoned to herself. In spite of Karen's promised publicity and the debate this week's issue of *The Red and the Gold* had fired up on campus, only the team — and Di and Elise — had turned up for the big event. The gymnastics team bus was half empty as usual. Half *full*, Katie corrected herself automatically. She had been trying for months now to practice the art of positive thinking. A small smile tugged at the corners of her mouth as she listened to Elise prattle on to Di about how absolutely exciting and scary it

111

was to be covering the meet this Saturday for the paper. She only wished she could feel as exuberantly cheerful as Elise. It was Elise's first stint as a stringer. True to her promise, Sasha was providing coverage of all weekend sport events, major and minor, and she had run out of reporters. Elise had been assigned the girls' gymnastics meet up in Potomac so Diana had come along too. Katie was especially glad since her one usual fan, Molly, hadn't been able to make it.

She fingered the turquoise-and-silver earring she wore in her left ear. Molly had loaned it to her for the day. It was her most treasured piece of jewelry. Molly's note had said: "I've never lost an akido match while wearing this. Maybe it'll bring you luck, too. Wish I could be there."

She really needed to talk to Molly today because the real reason she had the blues was Eric. She had so badly wanted to ask Molly's advice, even though nothing bad had happened. She hadn't seen Eric since Thursday, the night of their crazy almost-argument down in the basement. He had called last night to remind her about their date for pizza at Mario's on Sunday. He had wished her luck and apologized for not being able to make the meet. Just before he'd said good-bye he had told her he loved her. Katie's knees had almost buckled hearing that, but she couldn't help feeling a bit let-down. She had wanted to be able to look into his eyes the first time he said it so she could look at him and say she loved him back.

After their conversation in the basement Thursday night, she didn't feel like she was walking on air anymore. She didn't feel light and floaty. She felt more like her supple legs were suddenly made of lead, and she couldn't figure out why.

Last night she'd had the strangest dream — she was walking on some kind of narrow ledge. One wrong step and she'd fall off. Eric was in the dream, but when Katie woke up, she couldn't remember exactly what he'd been doing there. She only remembered that falling off felt awful even though she never hit the ground. She also remembered being surprised that Eric wasn't there to catch her.

"K.C.?" Elise said hesitantly.

Katie looked up and blushed a little, embarrassed that she had been lost remembering such a sad dream, instead of paying attention to her friends. "Sorry, I was — " she started to say, then improvised, "I was thinking about my routine."

"Oh, then I shouldn't bother you." Elise looked worried.

Katie brushed aside Elise's concern. "Bother me. Bother me," she said. Her laugh sounded a little forced. "I can use the distraction." She patted her stomach and sighed. "Butterflies. I always get them before a meet."

"I can believe that," Diana commiserated. "The one public thing I've ever done — that absolutely awful, horrid, humiliating modeling stint over the holidays — made me so nervous I still get butterflies remembering it. I don't know how people like you ever go on and compete."

Katie's laugh was genuine this time. "Performers and athletes kind of get inspired by the audience. Right, Elise?"

113

Elise agreed readily. She had played one of the leads in a school production of *Oklahoma!* and had loved every minute of it. "It helps knowing you've got friends in the audience. I never understood how important a cheering section was until I got on that stage last December and my wig fell off," she remarked.

Katie rolled her eyes in sympathy. "Tell me about it. At least you two are here today. I wish more kids had turned up, though. It's a downer for the team," she said, looking around the bus.

"It is too bad more of our gang isn't here." Diana frowned.

"There are just too many events scheduled all at once this weekend," Elise pointed out.

Katie nodded. "Even my boyfriend couldn't make it."

"Boyfriend!" Diana and Elise cried in unison.

Katie winced and looked around, but no one seemed to have noticed. She couldn't help but blush a little as she told her friends about her budding relationship with Eric. "He actually has a swim meet this weekend and he won't be back until tomorrow. I really wanted him to be here."

Diana eyed Katie thoughtfully. "That's tough — both of you being into competitive sports — "

"And they're both the same season," Elise pointed out.

Katie smiled bravely. "The good point is, we're both pretty serious athletes, so we're alike in a lot of ways. It's good having someone who understands the way you think and feel." Saying that aloud, Katie suddenly wondered if that were true. Were they really alike? Did Eric really understand her? She wasn't sure if she understood him at all, the way he had half expected Chris to favor Greg because he was her boyfriend.

"Hmmm — " Diana propped her long legs on the back of the seat in front of her and considered Katie's words. "Being alike sometimes is just as hard as being different. Like now, you might not ever get a chance to see each other perform. I think that would bother me."

"It does bother me," Katie readily admitted. "But there's nothing either of us can do about it."

"I don't think *that's* the real problem at all," Elise declared. "What if you get to go to the states after today and Eric doesn't? What would that do to your relationship? Phoebe told me about things like that happening when a guy and a girl both try out for parts in a big stage production. When one gets the role, and the other doesn't. All that competition's hard on a relationship."

Katie's response was instant. She sat up straight and shook her head vehemently. "Eric wouldn't mind. I know he wouldn't. There's a good chance of that happening, too. The swim team is going into today's meet with hardly a chance to score high enough to get through to the second round of this weekend's competition, let alone to the states at the end of the month." After a moment's hesitation, Katie repeated firmly, "No, Eric wouldn't mind me winning."

Elise wasn't convinced. "But suppose the tables were turned."

Diana looked puzzled. "What do you mean?"

"That Katie and the gymnasts don't make the states and Eric does. Wouldn't that bother you, Katie?" Elise asked seriously.

Katie started to smile. What a crazy idea. The thought of not making the states had never entered her head. The smile froze on her face. Slowly Elise's comment began to sink in. If Eric won and she lost, Katie Crawford had no idea how she'd feel. Last week, if Eric had managed to strike her out, would she have felt as warm and loving toward him? In all honesty, Katie didn't know the answer.

"BRRRRINNNGGG!"

For the third time that Sunday afternoon, the phone rang. Katie stampeded into the kitchen beating her brothers to it, and when she picked up the receiver it still wasn't Eric. "For you!" she growled in Danny's direction and fought back the urge to cry. Yesterday at Potomac she'd scored a perfect ten, and she couldn't wait to tell Eric. She couldn't wait to tell him how much she wished he had been there. Katie knew she'd never score a perfect ten again, and he had missed it.

"Sisters!" Danny rolled his huge brown eyes expressively and grabbed the phone from Katie's hand. He made a big deal about waving her away for privacy, even though it was just another one of his friends from Crestwood Elementary calling about next week's fourth-grade trip to the National Air and Space Museum. Katie was too disappointed to respond to her brother's teasing. She exhaled loudly and dragged her feet down the hall into the living room where she plopped herself in front of the TV to watch some reruns.

Feeling so let down each time the phone rang

didn't make sense. First of all, Eric had said he wouldn't be back in Rose Hill until Sunday night. It wasn't even four o'clock yet. Besides, whether she talked to Eric or not, Katie should have been feeling like the A-Number-One person in the whole town of Rose Hill because of her perfect ten. In spite of her gloomy mood, her growing sense of unease about Eric, and Elise's question rolling round in her head, she had given the best gymnastics performance of her life.

Katie sank a bit further into the plush cushions of the living-room sofa trying to get comfortable, but it was impossible. She'd woken up this morning suddenly knowing the main reason she did so well at the meet was Eric. And not because she was inspired by loving him; nothing as sweet as that. She had wanted to beat Eric, even though he had nothing at all to do with the competition. It wasn't Cindy Morgan, or Sara Weiss, or any of the girls on the Potomac High team she was competing against. It was that crazy, haunting picture of Eric in her head. What if Eric somehow made it to the states in the swim events, and she goofed up, got a lousy score, and ended up leading her team not to victory but to defeat? Mentally competing with him had spurred her on to an extremely impressive performance. It seemed weird to think of the guy she loved as a rival, and it definitely threw her off balance. Katie gave an annoyed toss of her head and tried to push aside the picture of herself as some kind of fierce competitor who didn't ever want her guy to win. But she knew inside she wasn't like that, or at least until now, she had always thought so.

Katie bit her already short nails, then commanded herself to stop. She picked up the remote control and began switching TV stations. A huge blue bird flapped its wings on a nature show; a Sunday preacher shouted loudly; a soppy thirties romance movie whizzed by. Nothing looked remotely interesting. She pressed the "off" switch and jumped up. Katie crossed over to the window and gazed dully at the sun-drenched lawn, trying to recapture the wonderful feeling of spring and falling in love, and how simple and clear everything had been when she had been in Eric's arms just a week ago. She hadn't been thinking of meets or winning or rivals then.

"So how's my little champion doing?" her mother asked, walking into the room.

Katie turned around and shrugged. "I'm bored. I wish I could go to the gym," she said, only half joking. Coach Muldoon and Mr. Romanski were in agreement on one point at least: after a major meet, Katie was to take one whole day off. It was a rule Katie usually loved keeping, but today she had so much excess energy.

"I've got a bit of a problem," Mrs. Crawford said, ruffling her fingers through her short, curly red hair. She looked worried. "I promised Will and Danny we'd go out to the miniature golf course if it got sunny." She looked out the window and grimaced at the brilliant, cloud-free sky. "Now I can't go. Mrs. Jenkins called and the local Greenpeace chapter is having a meeting. . . ."

Katie didn't give her mother a chance to finish. "I'll do it." She surprised herself by volunteering, but suddenly she didn't like the picture of herself moping around the house, waiting breathlessly by the phone. No wonder Danny had spent half the afternoon teasing her. She deserved it. Mooning around like a lovesick, confused romance heroine just wasn't her style. Chauffeuring her kid brothers to a round of putt-putt would get her out of the house and help take her mind off Eric, at least until she saw him tonight.

"I told you! It's my lucky earring." Molly Ramirez bounced up and down on the tips of her toes and pointed to the stud Katie was still wearing in her left ear. "See, Ted!" She pointed proudly to her good-luck charm and then squeezed Katie's hand. "I'm so happy for you. I just wish I could have been there."

Ted laughed heartily and gave Katie a warm hug. "Congratulations. Everyone is talking about your perfect ten!"

Katie hugged Ted back, then leaned her elbow on the roof of the enchanted gingerbread castle at Carrolton's Fantastic Planet miniature golf course. She was glowing with pride. Molly and Ted turning up here this afternoon had really made her day. Sharing her victory with good friends suddenly made it seem real — not like a magical, slightly out-of-focus dream.

"I wish you had been there, too," Katie concurred warmly. "But Di and Elise were. That's two more fans than usual." In spite of her good spirits, Katie sounded wistful. She didn't say she wished Eric had been there. Molly and Ted knew why he hadn't come. Molly sensed how she felt.

Molly tugged Katie's ponytail. "Hey, don't

worry. For the states in Annapolis, the whole Kennedy pep squad is going to tear the arena apart. Just you wait."

"It'll be too late, then," Katie said a bit morosely. "Don't forget, good student turnout is one of those 'facts and figures' determining who gets more funding next year. There was absolutely no crowd from Kennedy this weekend. No one."

"True, true. But it's the year's attendance they're looking at. Chris is probably poring over her friends, but Eric might be trying to reach her a short laugh. "Besides, everyone is talking about how angry they are they missed your show." Ted shouldered his golf club and guided Katie and Molly over to the Turbulent Tower of Evil. Molly's ball was trapped in a little sand pit guarded by a gaudily painted robot-dragon. Katie's was halfway across the drawbridge. Ted's was trapped in the top tower.

Before putting her ball, Katie looked around for her brothers. Will and Danny had already made their way once around the course and were heading across the parking lot to the food concession. Katie waved her club at them and motioned toward the car. She was enjoying her talk with her friends, but Eric might be trying to reach her by now, and she wanted to head home soon.

"Too bad the swim team screwed up as badly as they did," Molly mused, waiting for Katie to drive her ball over the bridge.

Katie's head snapped up. "The swim team?"

"Yeah, some of the guys were drowning their sorrows in subs — OUCH!" Ted flinched as Molly poked him in the ribs and groaned at his pun.

"They got knocked out of the competition yesterday in the first round and got back to Rose Hill this morning. I hear Eric was really in Doomsville, he was so upset about the loss. He had already left by the time we got to the sub shop."

Katie's heart stopped. Eric had been back all day and he hadn't called her. She felt like someone had just dumped a pail of ice water over her head. "Wow!" she said under her breath. "I don't believe it." She was surprised to feel tears welling up in her eyes. Katie never cried in front of anyone. The thought that she might horrified her, so she dropped down to the ground and pretended to retie the laces on her hightops.

"Yeah, poor Eric," Ted continued, misinterpreting Katie's comment. "He had such hopes pinned on his team. I wish he wouldn't take things so hard. Some games you win, some you lose," the football captain said philosophically, then whacked his ball out of the tower and moved on to the next hole.

Molly reached out and grabbed Katie's arm. She pulled her down the white stone path behind a white watermill. "Hey, what's wrong?" she whispered, her voice full of concern.

Katie took a deep breath and met Molly's eyes. "I don't know. It's . . . it's Eric . . ." she stammered. She looked around quickly. Will and Danny were sitting on a picnic table drinking shakes. Ted was safely out of earshot, whistling Kennedy's Fight Song as he progressed smoothly around the little course.

"I — I'm a little confused about him. I know he likes me," she said, then suddenly didn't want to continue. Talking to Molly had seemed like such a good idea. But now, facing the possibility that maybe Eric didn't like her, that after their talk Thursday he had thought things over and felt she wasn't the kind of girl he could be interested in, hurt too much to confide in Molly. Knowing that Eric had been home all day and hadn't called to ask her about her meet upset her even more. Katie gave an involuntary shiver. "I'll talk to you later, Molly. But not now. It's not a good time," she said, managing to keep her voice steady, though her heart was pounding very fast, and she suddenly felt scared.

She remembered her dream again — the one where Eric wasn't there to catch her when she was counting on him for support. Katie used to have a dream like that when she was a kid, after she'd taken her first bad fall off the bars and broken her arm. Her spotter hadn't been there to catch her. It was a silly accident but it took ages to get her confidence back. But she still dreamed about being in high places and falling. She wondered why Eric had turned into the spotter in her dreams.

"Katie," Molly suggested after a long silence, "sometimes it helps to talk."

Katie nodded. "I know. There's nothing to talk about now." But the rest of the way around the winding Fantastic Planet course, she wondered about falling in love. So far it wasn't quite all it was cracked up to be. Maybe she had made a mistake by letting Eric become more to her than just a friend. If a friend forgot to phone, it never felt as bad as this.

Chapter
12

Chris's hands trembled as she stacked the neatly typed sheets of paper on the podium. She purposely avoided the eyes of everyone sitting in the front row of Kennedy High's auditorium. She pulled the mike toward her and mumbled the usual words about exiting in an orderly fashion, not leaving soda cans, and a vague announcement about a baroque wind quartet performing for music assembly next week. As usual, no one listened. Today the decibels in the packed room were even more deafening than usual.

At the end of her presentation, Chris looked down from the stage into the sea of students. "Well, this is it," she sighed heavily. There was no back way out. Chris would have to face her friends and confront Greg.

Phoebe was the first to reach her. She was waiting right there at the bottom step, looking very proud. Chris searched her friend's sparkling green eyes a moment, then smiled hesitantly. "Was it all right?"

Phoebe giggled, confused by seeing the usually confident Chris looking so unnerved. "Chris, I think you did a really good job. I'm so glad girls' gymnastics is going to get more funds. Especially after that great performance Katie Crawford put on at Potomac. We might even place well in the states!" Phoebe prattled on excitedly.

Chris only half listened. She had heard about Katie and her performance after she had finished drawing up her charts and figures. A copy of the report was already lying on Principal Beeman's desk down the hall. The school board meeting was tonight. Chris felt proud of her work; she knew she had done a good job. But all pride and the sense of a job well done didn't make her feel very good inside. Greg had turned out the loser. The crew team just didn't merit the kind of support gymnastics, track, or swimming did. Chris had studied the figures for hours. She only hoped that maybe some bigwig on the school board would decide that in spite of the dismal statistics, crew was worth supporting.

"Coming to the cafeteria for lunch?" Phoebe asked. Chris realized guiltily she had missed the last five minutes of whatever her best friend had been talking about. Before she could reply, she spotted Greg.

He stood just inside the front exit door, towering over everyone. His cool blue-green eyes were fixed on her. Chris met his gaze, and her heart stopped. She had never seen him look so angry and so cold.

"Uh — not now," Chris stammered to Phoebe. Phoebe turned around and spotted Greg.

"Take it easy, Chris," she warned under her breath. "And good luck." With a couple of worried glances back over her shoulder, Phoebe exited the nearly empty auditorium by the rear door, leaving Chris and Greg up front, alone.

Chris squared her shoulders, and tucked her copy of the funding report in her bag. Then she headed directly toward Greg. She had no idea what she was going to say to him, though she had such a terrible lump in her throat she probably wouldn't be able to say anything at all.

Greg eyed her coolly as she approached, as if he were sizing up the height of a wave or the shape of a cloud out on Chesapeake Bay. He folded his long arms across his chest and shifted his broad shoulders uncomfortably. "Congratulations," he said. His voice dripped sarcasm.

Chris took a deep breath. "I'm sorry, Greg," she said very gently. She had done nothing wrong. She wanted him to realize that. He was hurt, and he had a right to be. His team was in trouble. She could feel for him, but she hadn't done anything wrong.

Greg arched his sandy eyebrows. "Sorry?" he repeated as if not quite understanding what she had said. The remote expression on his face didn't change. "I don't know why you should be sorry. You got back at me." As an angry flush stole up his neck, his eyes narrowed. "After all your talk about playing fair, you cut crew. You tried to kill the whole program. But you know what, Chris? I won't let you. Believe me, I won't."

He stared at Chris and shook his head in disbelief. "After all your talk about not letting personal matters interfere with your job. . . ." His bitter laugh rang out across the empty auditorium. Chris shrank back slightly. She could hardly believe that this was the same Greg she loved. He looked desperately cornered. Everything he believed in was threatened, and suddenly he sounded biting, cold, even a bit cruel.

"Well, you got even with me for our fight the other day. Just because you were angry, you cut my team."

"I what?" Chris gasped. "Greg, that's not true," she declared.

Greg dismissed her comment with a brusque wave of his hand. "Listen, you can get on the radio, get up there on the stage, and sweet-talk everyone else at Kennedy into believing you're playing fair, but you can't fool me. We won our first race on Saturday. Oh, it's not a big deal, not like gymnastics going to the states next week. But when you've graduated and you're out of this place, I'm going to get all the support crew will ever need. We're going to become the most talked-about team on campus next fall. Too bad you won't be around to see it."

Greg turned on his heel and started out the door. Chris ran after him, and planted herself in his path. She was livid. "You're actually accusing me of fixing the figures to get back at you because we didn't see each other this weekend? Because we had a fight Friday?" she cried.

Greg just stared at her in reply.

"Of all the nerve. You aren't *that* important to me that I'd do something like lowering myself to cheating!" she said, not knowing if she was making a bit of sense. "Just to get the record straight — " She glared at Greg with steely eyes. Her beautiful features were contorted with anger. " — All I did was assemble information for the school board. The figures are here in black and white. Anyone can check them." She waved her bag in Greg's face. "I'm not the one who cheated or was unfair. All along it's been you, Greg." She tapped him hard on the chest with her finger for emphasis. "All along, ever since the whole budget question came up, you've been pushing me to weigh the evidence in your favor. All you did was make my decision harder. And now you accuse me of cheating you! How dare you! How dare you stand there and act as if I'm the one slapping you in the face." Chris's words tumbled out one after another, running all together. Finally she stopped and gulped down some air.

"You said it, Ms. President!" Greg retorted angrily. "That's exactly what this whole thing feels like, a slap in the face." With that, Greg pushed through the exit doors and stormed down the corridor, around the corner, and out of sight.

Chris stood stunned, unable to move. Then her hand flew to her mouth, and she let out a sob. She stared down the hall. Greg was really gone. Slowly the thought sank in. She had never had such a terrible fight with anyone before. People didn't make up after fights like this. This time it was over. The funding crisis seemed like such a crazy thing to break up over. It didn't seem worth it. All this stuff about money and teams — what did that have to do with love?

Chris began to cry, first one tear then another

rolled down her cheek. She slid her back down the wall and sank onto the floor of the darkened auditorium. How could this be happening? How could Greg have talked to her like this? He had acted as if he hated her with all his heart and soul. She shuddered when she thought of the cold, angry way he had looked at her just now. He must believe she was the worst person in the world. Chris raked her fingers through her long hair. She had worn it today the way she knew Greg liked it best — half up, pulled back from her face in a wide blue barrett, and half down, flowing free and long to her shoulders. But obviously, Greg could not have cared less.

Chris leaned her head back against the wall and stared up at the high domed ceiling. Her tears subsided for a moment. She felt wrung out, used up. This had to be a terrible dream she'd eventually wake up from. She'd wake up and be back in bed, a light breeze blowing through the lacy curtains. Today wouldn't have happened yet. Chris rubbed her eyes with the backs of her hands, but the auditorium didn't go away. Muffled voices from the cafeteria drifted down the hall. She could hear the sound of a basketball thumping against the floor in the downstairs gym. This was no dream. Greg had accused her of terrible things. And the way he had looked at her, she knew in her heart there was no love left. "Oh, Greg!" Chris buried her face in her arms and cried.

Chapter
13

After assembly, Katie made her way down the cafeteria line with great difficulty. Kids she'd never seen before stopped to pump her hand, whack her on the back, and offer her loud congratulations on her stellar performance at Saturday's meet. Many voiced approval of Chris's decision to increase funds for girls' gymnastics. Katie reacted to the attention with a mixture of pride and confusion. She felt a little overwhelmed by the warm show of student support. Although she was ecstatic about her perfect ten and about leading the team to the states, she was still pretty depressed about Eric.

She had stayed up until midnight Sunday, but he had never called. Katie had no idea why he broke his promise. He had said on Friday that he'd call as soon as he got home. She had been so very sure then that he liked her. Last night, for the first time in years, she had cried herself to sleep. She hadn't done that since the day she had fallen flat on her face in front of the judges in the junior division regional championships.

She stood very still in the middle of the milling cafeteria crowd, remembering how kissing Eric felt. She took a deep breath and could still smell the chlorine in his hair. She could almost hear his voice, the special way he said her name. She had never liked her name before. She had thought it was so ordinary, so plain. But when Eric said it, it seemed like the most beautiful name in the world. Remembering his voice sent a shiver down her spine. Katie felt a funny catch in the back of her throat. She coughed, then crossed the cafeteria, heading for the crowd's table, thinking how much easier everything would be if she and Eric were just friends.

If he were one of her other friends, Katie would have picked up the phone last night and called. She could have asked him what had happened at the swim meet, and asked him why he hadn't called. But now she felt shy and afraid. What if he hadn't called because he didn't love her anymore?

"Three cheers for K.C.!" Woody Webster cried. The rest of the crowd gathered around the Formica-topped table greeted Katie with a round of applause. Phoebe patted the seat next to hers, and Katie gratefully dropped into a chair.

"Thanks, guys!" Katie said with a nervous laugh, wishing everyone would stop making such a big fuss. "I just hope everyone isn't too let down by whatever happens at the states. It's going to be pretty hard to live up to this buildup." Her eyes darted around the table. Eric wasn't there. She looked down at her tray and took a deep breath. Suddenly her lunch didn't look very appetizing.

"Let down? You couldn't let us down if you tried," Jonathan said. He reached over to Fiona's plate and plucked one of the radishes off her salad. He popped it in his mouth and munched it noisily. "Katie, even if Kennedy comes out last in the states, the point is you brought us there. No one's going to forget that."

"Besides, Katie couldn't come out last in anything!" Molly said loyally.

"My sentiments exactly." Woody thumped the table with the handle of his knife and looked as if he was about to start another round of cheers.

Seeing the look of dismay on Katie's face, Phoebe quickly intervened. "Give her a break, Webster. Let her eat her lunch in peace."

Woody retreated sheepishly behind his overstuffed pastrami sandwich.

"I think Katie should save her comments for one of Karen's interviews," Dee commented, thoughtfully munching a carrot stick.

Karen shoved her glasses on top of her head and leaned toward Katie. "In fact, I was thinking of having a once-a-week on-air sports interview for the rest of the season. Would you like to be my first guest?"

Katie agreed hesitantly. "Not until after the states though!" she added. "Why not interview Tara or Eric next?" Katie was surprised at how smoothly she managed to say Eric's name.

"Actually, too bad you interviewed Greg already," Kim commented. "I'd love to hear his reactions to crew's funds getting cut so drastically. It's really a shame."

"Not everyone could get an equal share of the money," Jonathan said. "Chris did a great job — and I know it was hard for her." All last week the student activities director had been working on the sidelines trying to help Chris get some of her facts and figures together before the weekend. Jonathan knew what a mess the "minor" sports were in. He was very impressed with the way Chris had handled the job.

"It is too bad about crew, though," Dee said slowly. "I was looking forward to watching the girls row next year."

"Oh, I wouldn't write off the crew team or Greg Montgomery just yet," Jonathan said with a knowing laugh. "Before Chris even finished reading that report, he told me he was going to request a review."

"What would that do to the rest of the budget?" Katie asked, suddenly worried. As upset as she had been about Eric, she had been extremely happy for him and the swim team. In spite of their poor showing over the weekend, they had been assured enough money for the coming year.

"I wouldn't worry about that if I were you," Fiona said. "With all the publicity gymnastics is getting since your terrific meet, Kennedy can't afford to cut back on it now."

Katie hadn't quite thought of it like that. "But I am sorry about crew," she said with a frown.

"I almost think Chris was being a little too fair," Kim said in passing.

Woody grimaced. "That's just what I was thinking. I can't quite believe boys' swimming is that much more popular than crew. Of course, I must admit I wouldn't get near boats or water with a ten-foot oar!" Woody was actually a good swimmer, but he habitually made fun of his awkwardness at most sports. He really did hate boats.

"I agree!" Molly said firmly. "I think crew deserved a better shake. I don't blame it on Chris. I just think it shouldn't have been up to her to make the decision. The school board should have done its own survey. Karen was right about it being unfair to Chris to have her involved so — intimately."

Phoebe frowned. "I think Chris did a great job in an impossible situation. I'm sure she did exactly what she felt was fair."

"Speaking of Chris," Jonathan looked around the room, "where is she?"

Phoebe caught her breath. Last time she saw Chris, Greg was there, looking very angry. Phoebe climbed up on her chair and looked around the crowded cafeteria. She spotted Brenda, sitting with Matt Jacobs and Pamela Green at a nearby table. Chris wasn't with them. Brenda caught Phoebe's eye and mouthed "Where's Chris?" with a puzzled expression on her delicate face.

Phoebe mimed back that she didn't know and jumped down from her chair. "Well, folks," she said, wrapping up the remains of her sandwich to throw away. "I've got a million things to do before next period." She gave a nervous tug on her thick red braid and tried to look casual as she left the cafeteria. The minute she hit the hall, she broke into a run. If her hunch was right, Chris was in trouble and probably needed a friend. But when Phoebe reached the auditorium, it was dark and empty.

Katie watched Phoebe's exit with envy. Smiling, laughing, and playing campus hero didn't sit well with her today. She appreciated her friends' support and attention, but at the moment she wanted to be alone.

She waited a discreet five minutes after Phoebe hurried out of the cafeteria, then excused herself from the table and mumbled something about errands to run and equipment to look at in the gym. She worked her way through the crowd and out the side door onto the quad.

It was a cool, damp day, and the frosty wind cut through her thin bowling shirt. Katie rubbed her upper arms and tried to figure out what to do, where to go. If the states weren't at the end of the week and if she didn't have to work out this afternoon, she'd cut all her classes and head home. In the three years she'd been at Kennedy, she had never done that. But Katie felt sore inside, sore and tender and very raw. She wanted to go home to her warm room and let herself cry. Not seeing Eric in the cafeteria at lunch had seemed like a kind of signal. Obviously he was avoiding her. Whatever the reason, their relationship was over. Katie suspected that the way she was feeling had something to do with a broken heart. She had wanted to learn all about love, but so far she wasn't sure love was something she wanted. Not if loving someone felt like this.

To keep warm, Katie started down the path

at a slow jog. Then she spotted his red jacket. He was down by the tennis courts with his hands jammed in his pockets. He was leaning against the gnarled trunk of a willow. Katie stopped running and just stood there watching a minute, not sure what to do. Eric must have sensed her presence. He turned around and looked up.

When he saw her, his face lit up with an incredibly happy smile.

Katie just stood there looking bewildered. A moment later he was by her side wrapping her in his strong arms. Katie wasn't sure how to respond.

She disentangled herself and took a couple of small steps back. She regarded him suspiciously. Deliberately, she put her hands in the pockets of her jeans. She didn't want to be tempted to touch him. "Eric, you didn't call," she said in a small, disappointed voice. "We were supposed to go to Mario's, remember?"

He stared at her blankly. Slowly the realization dawned on him. He slapped his hand to his forehead. "Last night. I was supposed to call. Oh, Katie — " he cried. "I'm sorry." He combed his fingers through his hair. It was wilder than usual and slightly frizzy from the damp air. Katie knitted her brow as she looked at him. He seemed distracted, worried about something.

She put a timid hand on his arm. "Eric? Are you okay?"

Eric flashed her a very unconvincing grin. "I'm fine," he said, then saw Katie didn't believe him. His whole body suddenly sagged. He gave a tight, sheepish laugh and look at his feet. "Okay, I'm not fine," he admitted finally. "I came back yesterday feeling pretty low. I went to the sub shop with the rest of the team. I should have called you then, I guess." When he looked back up at her, the sparkle was gone from his eyes. "I wasn't thinking much about anything. I just went home and fell into bed."

Katie dropped down beside him on a bench. The wood was damp, and she shivered slightly from the cold. She took Eric's hand and waited for him to go on.

"Uh, by the way, I did hear about your score at Potomac High. Congratulations," he said, almost as an afterthought.

"Thanks," Katie said, feeling a little let down. Eric sounded so absolutely unenthusiastic about her victory.

"At least one of us is doing our team justice," he remarked, a tinge of sarcasm in his voice. "Just when we needed to drum up student support, I let my team down in the relays. We didn't even make it to the finals against Virginia Prep!" Eric's self-disgust was evident.

"Oh, Eric, it wasn't your fault!" Katie protested, taking his broad, square hand between her two small ones. "Just because you're team captain doesn't mean winning is all on your shoulders. Besides, winning isn't everything," Katie said earnestly.

"I thought it was your favorite thing," Eric said in a quiet voice.

Katie caught her breath. She *had* said that. "It is," she admitted after a pause. "I love winning. But winning isn't what sports are all about.

Doing your best is. You know that." She reached up and tousled his hair.

An incredibly tender smile started across Eric's worried face. "Oh, Katie," he murmured. He leaned his head against her shoulder and let out a long sigh. "I just wish we had won on Saturday. I just wish I could do for my team what you do for yours."

Katie didn't know how to respond to that. Eric's remark unsettled her. So did the fact that he didn't exactly seem excited about her perfect ten. Katie forced down that thought. After all, he had just lost a very big meet. He didn't have the states to look forward to anymore. He was just down in the dumps. Katie drew him closer and began to massage a tense spot at the base of his neck.

"Hey, what are you doing after school?" he whispered into her ear.

"I've got a workout with Coach Muldoon," Katie said with a sigh. "Then another coaching session down at the Fitness Center." She debated with herself a minute before reminding him. "The states are at the end of the week."

He sat up straight and stared out over the wet lawn. "Oh," he said, sounding a bit flaky. "We sure have trouble getting to see each other, don't we?" he said sadly. "A guy could get the impression you weren't very interested."

"I can't help it. After this week it'll be easier." Katie nervously twirled the strap of her gym bag. She hadn't meant to give him the impression she was too busy to see him. She was busy, but somehow even a few moments together — like this —

were worth everything. "Eric, we can still see each other. How about between my coaching sessions today?"

Eric seemed appeased. "Okay. I'll meet you at the gym, four-thirty sharp," he said as the bell rang out across the quad. "Chemistry lab!" He leaped off the bench and pulled Katie up by his side.

"Study hall!" Katie groaned, wrapping her arms around him. They were in the middle of their second kiss, when the last tardy bell began to sound.

Reluctantly, Katie slipped out of Eric's embrace and raced him back to the main building.

Chapter
14

Slap. Thump. Slap. Thump.

When Phoebe heard the familiar sound of a ball hitting a racquet and rebounding off the wooden garage door, she relaxed a bit. "Chris?" she called, before rounding the corner of the stately Austin house and peeping into the back yard.

Chris had changed into a pair of soft pink sweats and had her hair pulled up in a tight, high ponytail. She turned to Phoebe, her eyes red-rimmed and puffy. But she wasn't crying now. The expression on her face was hard. Chris nodded curtly in Phoebe's direction, but didn't say hello. She bounced the yellow ball a couple of times on the pavement, then hit it fiercely with her racquet against the door.

Phoebe stood very still, just watching. Her first impulse was to run up to Chris, to hug her, to say everything would be okay no matter what awful thing had happened, no matter how bad things seemed now. But something about Chris practically shouted DO NOT TOUCH. Phoebe stood helplessly, her hands at her side, clutching her old purple knapsack by its frayed handle. She wasn't sure if she should stay or leave. Finally she sat down on the grass and waited for Chris to say something, to make the first move.

Chris's voice came out clipped and harsh as she finally broke the silence. "How did you find me?"

"I looked," Phoebe replied. "I looked everywhere. When you didn't turn up in French lit, I got kind of worried. I even checked the park." Ever since they were kids, Phoebe and Chris had had their own secret hiding place by the river in Rose Hill Park. When she hadn't found Chris there today, she got really worried. That was before she had thought of biking over to the Austins' to see if Chris had come home. Phoebe decided not to mention that she had seen Greg on the quad. From the look on his face, she knew something terrible must have happened between them.

"I had a fight with Greg," Chris said. She hit the ball as she spoke. "I needed some time to think. I figured Ms. Perfection could break a few rules herself every once and a while, so I came home." Chris caught the ball on its next rebound, and stood straight as a stick staring down at her tennis shoes. She took a deep breath and turned toward Phoebe. She struggled to say something, then shook her head dismally from side to side, pressing her palms to her temples. Her shoulders started shaking before the first tear fell.

Phoebe jumped up and a second later was by her side. "Oh, Chris. It must hurt so much!" she cried. She made Chris face her.

In a halting, broken voice Chris recounted the whole scene with Greg. As Phoebe led her to the back porch, Chris wailed, "He was so mean, Pheeb. And he really believed I fixed the figures to get back at him. I thought he knew me better than that. I really did. . . ."

Phoebe sat down on the wide porch and pulled Chris down beside her. She unearthed some crumpled tissues from the pockets of her overalls and handed them to Chris, then struggled to think of something to say — some words of advice. Nothing came to her. She had seen the anger on Greg's face, and she had a terrible sinking feeling that Chris and Greg were beyond fixing.

Chris sniffed and blew her nose. "I'll show you. I'll show you everything; all the figures, all the work I did. Oh, Phoebe, I didn't cheat him. I didn't try to get back at him. I tried as hard as I could not to think of him all weekend," Chris insisted. She led Phoebe up to her room.

Phoebe knew Chris would never consciously cheat anyone, but she didn't understand how crew could have lost *all* of its funding. Lots of people were beginning to talk about that. But now, looking at the carefully penciled calculations, Phoebe had to admit Chris had done an incredible job. All those facts and figures were mind-boggling: information gathered through interviews with students, a year's worth of attendance lists for each sporting event, press releases, clippings from local papers. Chris had been absolutely thorough and fair. She looked up from the sheets of yellow paper and said, "Chris, if Greg could see this, I know he'd change his mind."

"Well, forget it. I'm sure he'll never talk to me again, and I don't particularly want to talk to him, either," Chris said in a shaky voice.

Phoebe kicked off her sneakers and crossed her legs under her on the bed. She waited for Chris to get hold of herself, then began in a slow, cautious voice, "Chris, I think you were fair and did a very good job. But I am your friend, and I have to be honest."

Chris's shoulders tensed and a flicker of suspicion crossed her face. "What are you getting at? You just said it all looks fair."

"It is fair. But I think maybe you were being a little *too* fair. Is it possible you bent over backward to keep from playing favorites?"

"How can you say such a thing? It's all right here!" Chris jumped up from her desk chair and crossed the floor to the bed. She ruffled through a stack of pages. "Here, look. Crew scored lowest on all counts: attendance, support, number of kids who participate in the sport, and actual economic need."

Phoebe stood her ground. "Right. By about two points, Chris. Two points behind guys' swimming, three points behind girls' track and field. The only clear winner is girls' gymnastics. I think you could have at least let crew keep what funds it had and not given gymnastics quite so much. You still would have been fair."

"You mean that? You really think I bent over backward not to favor Greg?" She flopped down on the bed next to Phoebe and stared at the ceiling. Then she sat up, pushed her hair off her face and aimlessly began braiding and unbraiding her ponytail.

She faced Phoebe. "I've made a terrible mistake, Pheeb. What can I do about it now?" Her trembling voice sank to a whisper, and she reached for Phoebe's hand.

"I don't know," Phoebe admitted in a very sad voice.

Chris got up and yanked some tissues out of the box beside her bed. She wandered over to the window. The sleepy afternoon street was coming to life: a school bus from Rose Hill Country Day School stopped across the way, depositing the neighbor's four-year-old on the sidewalk. "The school board meets tonight," Chris said in a flat voice. "I can't change anything before then." She shrugged her shoulders in despair. "There's no helping Greg now. I can't make things right."

Phoebe fiddled with the straps of her overalls. "You know, Chris, I don't think you have to worry about helping Greg," she said. "He can take care of himself in the money department. I heard he's already requesting a review —"

Chris cringed. "Ugh!"

"And if that doesn't work, Jonathan told me he has another plan to raise money. You know how resourceful he is."

"Tell me about it." Chris smiled slightly.

"So fixing up your mistake isn't the real problem, Chris," Phoebe said. "You've got to figure out what to do about Greg and you."

"Greg and me. Phoebe, after what he said —"

She bit her lip and corrected herself, " — after what *we* said, there's nothing I can do."

"You still love him," Phoebe said simply.

Chris caught her breath and started to deny it. Her shoulders sagged slightly, and she leaned back against the pale, flowered wallpaper. "I do still love him, Phoebe. You're right. But what can I do about it now?"

Phoebe slowly shook her head back and forth.

"I don't know what you can do, Chris. But I know if you love him, you'll figure it out somehow. Love always works like that." She thought of her and Michael and the good times and tough times they'd had since last summer. The one thing she was sure of was that love always worked.

"How about that famous smile!" a photographer yelled from his perch on a bench. The minute the afternoon workout was over, the local press had descended on the Kennedy High gym, eager to interview the girl from Magnolia Street who had scored a perfect ten.

Katie turned in his direction and blinked as the flashbulb went off. Spots and dots danced in front of her eyes, but she kept smiling anyway. Part of her job just then was to be gracious and try not to make a fool of herself answering questions. Ms. Muldoon had practically drilled her on how to treat "the press" when they turned up after practice. Newspaper coverage was good publicity and good publicity could only help her team right now. Katie caught Ms. Muldoon's eye and cleared her throat and began to answer the reporters' questions as best she could. Between the lights and the flashbulbs, she didn't see Eric walk in.

"Katie," one reporter asked, "Where do you go after the states?"

Katie blinked her huge brown eyes and looked bewildered. "After the states?"

"Do you plan to start competing on a national level? How about the Olympics?"

Katie's laugh was instant, her smile natural and warm. "No way!" She shook her head adamantly and paused to yank up her leg warmers. "I'm too old!" She giggled and everyone joined in. Encouraged by the friendly faces, Katie confided in a more serious voice, "High school competition is more my style. Being an Olympic champion means giving up almost everything. I like school and my family and friends too much for that. It takes a different kind of person."

"So you'll be happy just to win in the states?" The reporter didn't quite sound convinced.

"Just to win the states?" Katie repeated incredulously. "That would be great. However I do — however the team does in the states, I'm proud to be going to Annapolis to represent Kennedy High. We're the only Kennedy team that made it to the state level and I'm honored to be part of it."

Eric stood off to the side, his stomach churning. He couldn't believe Katie had just said that. He felt like she had punched him in the gut. But his next thought was, what was the matter with him? Katie's going to the states should make him proud.

Katie was handling this interview like a real

pro. But somehow seeing her look so comfortable, so at ease in front of all those photographers and reporters, bothered him. Watching her bask in the glory of her success made him feel as if he had really failed his team. Thanks to Katie, the girls' gymnastics team had made it to the top level of competition in their sport. But as much as Eric admired her for that, he envied her, too. He felt that he should have been able to push himself harder so he could be standing there alongside her, talking about what a great bunch of athletes Kennedy's swimmers were.

The minute the interview was over Eric glanced up at the clock. Five-thirty. "It's late!" he said, as Katie ran up smiling with her gym bag under her arm.

Katie frantically looked at the clock and groaned. "Oh Eric," she wailed. "I have to get right over to the Fitness Center. My lesson is at six-fifteen."

Eric stared at her. "What about us?" he said. His voice held a note of a challenge in it.

Katie tilted her head and looked at him, surprised. "Uh, well, we'll have to put it off until another night. I'm sorry, Eric. The interview wasn't my idea. I didn't know a thing about it."

"No, I guess not," Eric grumbled and kicked the base of the spectator stands. He shoved his hands in his pockets and looked around the room, then ran his fingers through his hair nervously.

"You know, I'm beginning to get the feeling you can't fit me into your life these days."

"What are you talking about? I've got the states coming up in a couple of days. I've got extra training sessions. You wouldn't expect me to give all that up just to — " Katie faltered. "Just to go out. I mean, the season's over *next week*, Eric."

"Don't be ridiculous," he said, a little too quickly. "I don't want you to give anything up." He paced away from Katie, then back again. "I just get the feeling you have no time to spend with me right now. All that matters is you and this competition and — "

"No time to spend with you!" Katie responded angrily. "You haven't had time for me, either! You couldn't come and see my meet on Saturday."

"You didn't come to my meet, either," Eric retorted. He paused for a moment and took a deep breath. "Oh, Katie, what are we doing?"

They stared at each other long and hard. Suddenly Katie tilted her head to the side and squinted. Eric looked so scared and a little confused. One clump of hair stood up straight from the top of his head and she wanted to reach out and smooth it down. He looked so sweet and silly standing there. She struggled to contain the laughter rising to her lips.

"Is this our first fight?" she asked, dumping her bag on the bench and sitting down with a thump.

Eric plopped down next to her. His smile was a bit slow in coming, but he nodded. "I think so."

Katie impulsively reached out for his hand. "How about if I come to your next meet?"

"You can't," Eric stated solemnly. "It's Friday, the night before your big meet in Annapolis."

"Oh." Katie's face fell. She had really wanted to see him.

"But I'll tell you what. I'll come to yours. When is it?"

"Wednesday. A tumbling competition." Katie's eyes glowed at the prospect. She always won tumbling matches. Then she clapped her hand to her forehead. "And, of course, there's the states on Saturday. You'll be there?" Katie held her breath waiting for Eric's reply.

But he said nothing, just stared dreamily into her wondering eyes, and tilted her chin up. "Does that mean yes?" Katie teased, as his lips neared hers. Eric just smiled and sealed his promise with a kiss.

Chapter
15

On Wednesday afternoon, Coach Mitchell's shrill whistle echoed throughout the pool area to signal the end of practice. Eric ignored the sound and pushed off the side for one last lap. The coach's pre-workout pep talk had really inspired him. Not making the states this season was over and done with. Each member of the team was a fine athlete and had no reason to be ashamed of his performance. Now the team's business was to make the last couple of races count and get a head start on next season, physically and psychologically —to break for the summer on a winning streak.

Keeping the coach's words in mind, Eric was aiming to top his personal best in the butterfly. By Friday, he wanted to push the clock a second faster.

Eric hoisted himself out of the pool, removed his noseguard, and pulled out his earplugs. When the coach approached him with a towel, he was dripping on the white tiled floor.

"Good work, Eric," Coach Mitchell said. Eric was pretty winded, but he managed to acknowledge the coach's remark with a tired smile. The coach wasn't the sort to say much, but Eric could read approval in his steady gaze. Eric had never worked harder than he had today. For the first time in months he felt proud of himself. It was amazing what a little inspiration could do. He had been psyched up not just by the coach, but by Katie's example. Maybe if he had worked this hard all year, the swim team would be in a different position today. He pushed the thought from his mind and reminded himself it really didn't matter now. The coach's mellow voice interrupted his reverie.

"I'd appreciate it if you'd sort of lead the ranks in that program with Garfield House. I posted a sign-up sheet in the locker room. No one had signed it the last time I looked. Maybe if the captain leads the way. . . ."

Eric looked puzzled a moment, too tired to remember exactly what the coach was talking about. "Oh, those Saturday swim programs for the halfway house kids." Brenda Austin had come to the pool and made the announcement before practice started. A pilot sports program involving students from Kennedy High with Garfield House residents was in the works. Opening the Kennedy pool and giving basic swimming instruction, plus courses in lifesaving and water safety, would be the first of many efforts to help the halfway house kids reorient themselves to the community and school environments. Eric thought it was a great idea. "Don't worry. I'll get more guys than you'll know what to do with," he promised.

"Maybe they'll be more enthusiastic when they hear there's a girls' sign-up list, too." The coach laughed and headed back to his office.

Eric wrung the water out of his hair and squeaked his way across the wet floor to the locker room. The sign-up sheet was posted on the inside door. Hanging nearby was a pencil on a string. Coach Mitchell was right. Not one guy had signed up yet. Without reading the notice, Eric scrawled his name on the top line, and bellowed into the steamy room, "Hey, guys, get over here. The coach needs volunteers. Am I going to have to volunteer you?" After a dramatic pause he added rakishly, "There's a girls' sign-up list, too."

Groans and protests met Eric's threat. Eric silently started counting to ten. Before he reached five, Danny Otis, Chip Mendez, Dick Mosely, and Robby Samuelson had filed up and penned their names beneath Eric's. Eric grinned. The coach was right. Telling the guys about the girls' being there worked.

Eric was in front of his locker, when Danny's voice rang out from the next aisle. "Just the way I wanted to spend this Saturday — in the pool." He let out a dramatic groan. Someone else made a remark about how Danny usually spent his Saturdays, but Eric didn't hear a thing. He stood stunned, a towel around his waist, his combination lock in his hand.

Saturday. This Saturday was Katie's meet —

the big one — the states. And he had just signed up for a Garfield House swim session. For a moment, he considered the idea of walking over to the list, picking up the pencil, and erasing his name. But something stopped him. He was the captain. He couldn't do that. He couldn't tell everyone else to turn up Saturday, then cop out himself. And he had promised the coach.

Eric pounded his fist against the next locker, then turned around and leaned against the cold metal. He folded his arms across his chest and stared up at the acoustical tiles in the ceiling. Why lie to himself? He hadn't bothered to read the notice before signing the coach's list, but he had heard the announcement just like everyone else before practice began. He had forgotten all about it. When the coach mentioned it just now, he was waterlogged, winded, and exhausted. He hadn't remembered the session was this Saturday. He really and truly hadn't, and yet, he was suddenly convinced that deep down inside he had known. Because every time he thought of going to the states Saturday, his stomach knotted up. He didn't want to go to the states. He didn't want to be there for Katie's big meet. The idea of her in the limelight, him on the sidelines, drove him crazy.

Eric pressed his hands hard against the side of his forehead, as if he could squeeze some sense into his brain. Nothing was making sense now. Nothing had made sense at all since he met Katie. He wasn't quite sure loving someone was supposed to make sense, but loving someone should make him feel good, not jealous and angry. He had never loved anyone the way he was beginning to love Katie Crawford. Just thinking of her now, his heart started thumping in his chest and he felt this crazy, happy feeling. Being with her he could be silly, he could laugh, act like a little kid again, do dumb stuff like roller-skate. He could make a fool of himself and not care. Because whatever he did, it was okay with Katie. She'd love him anyway. It was the same way he felt about her, most of the time.

But then someone like Ted or Marc would say something to him about Katie's perfect ten, about how great an athlete she was, about her leading her team single-handedly to the states, and the crazy, happy feeling would turn to lead. His insides would start churning, and he didn't know why. He felt like he was in some kind of race with her to prove who was best, who was tops. The worst part was that he knew in his heart it was a race he couldn't possibly win. As an athlete, Katie outclassed him. And Eric was having a heck of a time accepting that.

"Hey Shriver, need a ride home?" Chip called from the hall door.

"Huh?" Eric said dully. His eyes sought the clock. Four forty-five. He suddenly snapped to attention, remembering Katie's tumbling match. He was late. "Uh, no!" Eric shouted in Chip's direction and raced for the shower stalls.

He showered just long enough to rinse off the pool water, then pulled on his jeans and buttoned his shirt as he tore down the hall to the gym.

He flung open the door and watched in dismay as Katie finished her last backflip across the mat and landed with a solid thump, square and strong

153

on both feet, her arms raised in an exultant pose. The small crowd burst into applause. Katie smiled broadly as she bowed. When she straightened up she saw Eric, standing there in the doorway trying to catch his breath with his shirt buttoned all crooked. The smile froze on her face. Eric shifted his glance away from hers. He could tell from the look on her face she knew he had turned up way too late.

Eric was sitting outside the girls' locker room, just like Katie knew he would. She stood in the doorway and shuffled her feet, trying to decide what to do. With her mind made up, she steeled herself and marched up to Eric. He didn't see her coming.

"You missed it, didn't you?" she accused, planting herself right in front of him. She was wearing her green-and-black football jersey with the tiny hole under the arm, the one she had worn the first time he kissed her. The strap of her denim overalls was falling off her shoulder, but she didn't seem to notice it until Eric reached out on impulse to pull it up. Katie took a quick step backward and yanked it up herself. She looked very hurt.

Eric cleared his throat. "Practice went late," he said, shifting his gaze away from Katie.

Katie looked intently at Eric. She knew about practices and coaches. She started to tell him that, but she could see something else was wrong. "I'm sorry about that," she said. She dropped her bag to the floor and struggled into her yellow slicker. She kept her eyes on Eric the whole time, waiting for him to say something, to explain why he couldn't meet her eyes. "Eric," she said impatiently and checked her watch. She was due at the Fitness Center in another hour. "I'm really upset you missed the match, not because it was any great shakes, but because you said you'd be there. I kind of counted on you. . . ." Her voice trailed off. Being let down like this hurt.

"I know," Eric said sullenly. "I know you did. And I'm sorry. I couldn't help it."

"Okay." Katie made a conciliatory gesture with her hands. "It's not such a big deal. What really matters is Saturday, the states. You are coming to Annapolis, aren't you?"

Eric looked up and shook his head miserably. "I can't."

"You can't?"

"The swim team, something came up. The coach asked for volunteers for the Garfield House sports program. I wasn't thinking and I signed up. It's Saturday. This Saturday."

"Can't you un-sign up?" Katie asked, not willing to believe what was happening. "So you made a mistake with the date — Coach Mitchell will understand that. There will be other Saturdays, other times you can help the kids at Garfield."

"Don't you understand," Eric retorted defensively, "I'm the team captain. I can't con everyone into signing up and giving up their own Saturday, then presto" — he snapped his fingers — "just back down because my girl friend wants me to go to a gymnastics competition."

"Because *I* want you to be at my meet? That's why you're coming to see me — you *were* coming

to see me?" she corrected pointedly. "I don't believe this." Katie glared at Eric. "I should have
known. You have absolutely no desire to see me
win or lose. For some reason, watching me go
out there doesn't interest you one bit, does it?"

"Come off it, Katie. You haven't exactly been
hanging around the pool, either!" Eric snapped.

"No. But first chance I got after Saturday, I
was going to. *I* wanted to see you swim. *I* wanted
to cheer you on. Is that such an abnormal thing
for a girl to want to do for a guy she — she cares
about? Is it such a crazy thing to want you to be
there when I go to the biggest meet of my life?
Is it?" Katie gulped, trying to force back the terrible urge to cry. "In fact," she accused angrily,
"I think the real reason you won't be there Saturday is because you're jealous. You didn't make
the states and I did." Katie blurted out the words
in anger, not really meaning them. Her next words
died on her lips. One look at Eric's face, and she
realized she had hit on the real problem. The
pain and betrayal she felt about him standing her
up had vanished. Suddenly she was horrified and
scared. She gasped. "I'm right!" she gasped. "You
think you're competing with me somehow." As
she said that, she suddenly remembered her own
feelings in Potomac last Saturday, the way she
had tried so hard because she didn't want Eric
to outdo her in his meet at Virginia Prep. "Oh,
wow!" She leaned back against the concrete wall
and tried to digest what was going on.

But Eric didn't give her a chance. She had
struck a raw nerve and something in him lashed
out. "How can you call me competitive?" he said

bitterly. "You're the one who has to play a dumb softball game as if it's the last inning of the last game of the World Series."

"And you're such a bad sport you still resent me winning that game, two weeks later," Katie fumed. "Well, you can keep your jealousy and resentment, because I don't need it. I don't need someone like you. Someone who expects me to lose or to do less than my personal best so his ego doesn't get wounded. No, I don't need that at all." She picked up her bag and slung it over her shoulder. Glaring at Eric one last time, she stormed off to the locker room, her heart pounding, her head throbbing, and her eyes stinging with tears. Only when she slammed the door behind her did she remember Eric was supposed to drive her to Georgetown, and it was too late to catch the last school bus.

Chapter
16

Katie went through the familiar motions of preparing for the vault. She mechanically tuned out all the distractions of her surroundings: the shouts of encouragement that Neva, Mr. Romanski's assistant, gave to the eight-year-olds practicing rudimentary floor exercises on the far side of the gym; Carla Mulroy's grunts and groans as she worked out on the uneven bars; the faint sound of Molly Ramirez's voice rising up through the stairwell from the akido studio downstairs; the persistent rain drumming on the roof of the Fitness Center.

Like a well-programmed windup doll, Katie began the same routine she'd done about a million times now over the past eight years. Keeping her back perfectly straight, she approached the faint chalk boundary precisely seventy-five feet from the horse. She turned around, lined her toes up flush with the marker, and flexed first her right foot, then her left. She clenched and unclenched her fists and shook the tension out of her wrists. Taking a deep breath, she stood perfectly still. Katie closed her eyes to prepare her mind for the vaulting sequence, beginning with the starting run, right to sticking the landing the way Mr. Romanski taught her. "Like glue — you land. *Kerplunk*. You don't move!"

But cool, calm, and collected as Katie looked on the outside, inside she was churning. Like a washing machine stuck in the spin cycle. She felt a fuzzy, blurred sort of pain, a combination of anger and hurt.

After her fight with Eric, she had blindly stumbled onto a city bus, only to arrive at her lesson a half-hour late. Mr. Romanski was fuming, but Katie barely heard his tirade. All she could hear was the sound of Eric's voice, the way he had reacted when she accused him of being jealous of her. She couldn't stop thinking of the competition between them. As much as he might love her, or she love him, beneath the surface they'd always be vying with each other to be number one. This time around he had let her down, but in his shoes, Katie had no idea how she would feel, or what she would do.

"Katherine Crawford, *what are you doing*?" Mr. Romanski's voice echoed through the gym. Except for the rain you could have heard a pin drop.

Katie gulped. "Nothing — " she stammered, and rubbed her palms against her bare thighs.

"Nothing?" he roared. "Nothing, and you're about to do your vault? You're thinking of nothing? Not your push off, your twist, your landing? Nothing!" This time one of the eight-year-olds over by Neva gave an hysterical giggle. Mr. Romanski whipped around, his dark eyes burning. "And what are you doing, Missy, what are you doing?" The girl ducked back behind Neva, who struggled not to smile.

Katie exhaled deeply and without a further thought, sprinted as fast as she could to the board then took off, punching her hands hard against the horse, twisting in the air. It was all wrong. She felt it before she completed the vault. Fortunately, when she landed, flat on her side, she had missed the horse by a couple of inches.

She lay there a minute, winded, waiting for Mr. Romanski to yell again. Instead he came up quickly, reached out a hand, and pulled her to her feet. "Katie, is there something wrong?" he asked, his gruff, accented voice suddenly soft and low.

Katie didn't answer. She tossed her hair off her face and massaged her right thigh. It still stung from where she landed.

"Katie, we work together many times a week. I know you like my own daughter, almost. I know you that many years. Something is different tonight — you're not just tired. You're in a dangerous frame of mind. Dangerous for doing gymnastics. Careless, lazy, no *oooomph*." He made a vague gesture with his hand and twirled his mustache.

He waited for Katie to say something. She looked around the room with her arms tightly crossed. Suddenly she felt chilled, and everything seemed blurry and out-of-focus.

"What is it?" He continued to probe.

"Nothing!" Katie replied shrilly. "Nothing's wrong. Even if something were wrong, I've never, ever let something personal interfere with my performance here. I never have and I never will." With that she stomped across the floor toward the dressing room.

"Katie?" Molly Ramirez was standing just inside the hall door, her red raincoat over her arm, her car keys in her hand. She had come upstairs to give Katie her usual Wednesday ride home.

Katie stared blankly at her friend, forgetting for a moment why she was there.

"What's wrong?" Molly tossed her coat on the registration desk and approached Katie cautiously.

Katie tried to say something, but seeing Molly's friendly face, she burst into tears.

Katie let Molly maneuver her into the changing room and onto a bench. "Did something happen just now with Romanski?" Molly asked quietly, stroking Katie's tangled hair.

"No," Katie whispered. "I mean yes. Oh, Molly, everything's so awful. Eric — Eric — " she couldn't go on. She hid her face in her arms and cried so hard she felt as if her insides were being torn out.

"Let's go somewhere," Molly said gently, handing Katie her clothes. "Somewhere we can talk."

Katie didn't remember saying yes or no to Molly. She was suddenly very tired and everything felt numb. She still felt like that, twenty minutes later, as she sat before a tall ice-cream soda in Sticky Fingers. She eyed the frothy ice-cream concoction skeptically, then pushed it away. She didn't want to eat, and she didn't want to talk to Molly. Talking wouldn't solve anything.

Molly regarded Katie with her round blue eyes and observed shrewdly, "Keeping all this to yourself won't help. You haven't told me one thing about you and Eric yet, except that you like him, and that you've been seeing him a lot. But something's wrong. Something's been wrong all along — "

When Molly said that, Katie sat up straight. "What makes you say that?"

Molly poked a hole in her ice cream and watched the hot fudge trickle into the crevice. She chose her next words carefully. "I just got a feeling. Eric's been looking awfully down lately. Everyone thought it had to do with the swim team not making the states. . . ." She let her voice trail off, waiting for Katie to volunteer information.

Her strategy worked.

At the mention of the word "states" Katie's whole body tightened. "He's not coming to the states on Saturday, Molly. He promised he would, and now he's going to be there. He wasn't at my meet today, either. And he had promised to come to that, too." Katie teetered on the brink of tears but forced herself to stay dry-eyed. It hurt to say that out loud, but saying it seemed to hurt less than keeping it in.

"The louse," Molly said instantly, stabbing her ice cream with her spoon. She shook her head and let out a long sigh. She met Katie's sad eyes

162

and admitted grudgingly, "But I'm not surprised."

"What do you mean?" Katie gasped. "You're the one who said he's such a great guy." Instantly she apologized. "Sorry, I shouldn't have said that. How could you know it wouldn't work?"

"K. C.!" Molly eyed her friend in disbelief. "It's not like you to give up so easily."

"Just forget it, Molly," Katie said, starting to shred her napkin. "There's no way the two of us can get together again. And you know what," she admitted, "I can't blame him, either. I don't know what I'd do in his shoes. If he were going to the states, and I weren't, I'd feel pretty crummy. In fact," she confided with great difficulty, "I think I got that ten because I wanted to be sure I won, in case Eric won that day, too." She anxiously peered into Molly's eyes, expecting her friend to look horrified.

Instead Molly started to smile, then struggled to keep a straight face. "So, what's new? That's you, Katie. You want to be tops. It's just who you are. Eric's the same. So am I, so is Ted, so is Marc. Chris Austin, too. Nothing's wrong with that. It's just the way it is. Look on the bright side, the guy inspires you."

"But loving someone should change all that!" Katie cried.

Molly shrugged. "I don't know. How can you change who you are? Maybe you just have to figure how you can want to be competitive with Eric, but love him at the same time."

Katie considered Molly's words. They made sense, but she still felt pretty hopeless. She shuddered remembering the way Eric had acted today.

163

"I don't know, Molly. It's just not in the stars, I guess."

"Stars, jars!" Molly said, dismissing Katie's comments with a wave of her hand. "It has nothing to do with the stars. It has to do with Eric's ego. All along, ever since that dumb softball game, all the guys have been razzing Eric about dating a higher-classed athlete than himself. They've been pretty ruthless. I think it got to him. Especially when he didn't lead his team to the states."

Katie leaned forward on her elbows. "And I did," she said more to herself than to Molly.

"He thinks the team failed because he somehow failed them," Molly concluded.

Katie nodded very slowly. "That sort of explains things, doesn't it? I mean, why he won't be there on Saturday to see me." Katie looked up at Molly, her eyes two pools of sadness. "To tell you the truth, I sort of figured all of that out already."

Having Molly say it out loud had helped, though. Katie felt less angry at Eric. He couldn't help who he was. Everything made more sense now. Katie's insides stopped churning, and by the time Molly drove her home, and she climbed the stairs to her room, her overall hurt and anger had faded to a dull ache.

She crawled into bed and pulled the blankets up over her head. Lying there in the dark, she tried to imagine herself as another kind of girl, a person who didn't care so much about winning, the kind of girl who took it for granted guys were better, stronger, braver. Was it worth learning to lose just to be with Eric? Katie hugged her

164

pillow to her chest and wished with all her heart as she lay there that competing wasn't such a part of her. For a fleeting instant she actually wished she had hurt herself when she fell tonight doing her vault. Then she wouldn't be able to make the match on Saturday.

She yanked off the blanket and bolted up in bed at that thought. She flicked on her light and pushed back her hair, still stringy and damp from the rain. She propped her chin on her knees and stared across the room at her poster-covered wall and felt a sudden wave of embarrassment as she faced the pictures of all of her heroines. "If they could hear me now," she whispered to the empty room.

She jumped out of bed and padded across the floor, clutching her baggy Orioles jersey tight across her chest. She walked right up to the picture of Mary Lou Retton and stared the triumphant gold-medalist right in the eye. Maybe Katie Crawford wasn't quite the stuff Olympic champions were made of, but she wasn't a loser, either. She was who she was — a fierce, determined girl who loved winning, who loved feeling every inch of her body come alive as she soared through the air in a perfect vault, or balanced precariously on the high bar. She could no more stand on the sidelines and watch than — than — Katie sank down to her dressing table chair and finished her thought. Than Eric Shriver. She couldn't not compete just for him. She had to go out there no matter how badly she felt and do her best. No matter who was watching and who wasn't. Even if winning meant losing the guy she loved.

Chapter
17

Greg tore a sheet of paper off the pad on his clip board. He balled it up and pitched it across the breadth of the living room, aiming for the white wicker basket near the rattan couch. Except for Greg, the stately Montgomery house was deserted tonight, and it was so quiet he could actually hear the light tap of the paper landing in the basket. A perfect shot. He should congratulate himself, he thought wryly, just like he should congratulate himself on the fine job he was doing securing the future of Kennedy's crew team.

In two days he had accomplished the impossible. He had done a month's worth of leg work. He had made a zillion phone calls and canvassed his heart out around the school and in town. Tonight alone he'd talked to Woody Webster, Jonathan Preston, Deputy Mayor Roselli, the American University crew coach, Kim Barrie, and Peter Lacey — everyone he knew who had clout or experience raising funds. Then he had called Jonathan again to give him the results of his little private survey: who would help him, who wouldn't, and exactly what could be done to save the crew team. So far his plans to save his team were panning out. Actually, they were more than panning out. According to his latest calculations, if a fund-raising drive raised half as much as Jonathan said it would, crew would end up with twice the funds it currently needed.

Tossing his clipboard on the low teak coffee table, Greg got up from his chair and began to pace the polished parquet floor. He strode restlessly from the fireplace, to the desk, the window, the big French doors, and back again. Like Jonathan had said, now it was time for the head work and the brainstorming. Time to concoct some crazy scheme to lure the good citizens of Rose Hill to part with their hard-earned dollars and enjoy themselves doing it. But, as he flopped back down on the sofa, stretching his long legs straight out in front of him, he knew as far as bright-new-ideas went, he might as well toss in his towel. Right now, the only idea in his head was Chris.

As long as he kept moving, kept himself busy, he was able to keep his mind off her. The minute he stopped and let himself think, like now, he remembered. He remembered everything about her, and it was torture, sheer torture. Greg took a deep breath. Maybe it was just the fragrance from the flowers in the antique vase by the phone where he sat, but he could almost smell the faint scent of the lily-of-the-valley perfume she sometimes wore. If he closed his eyes, he seemed to see her face: the way the determined set to her chin and her mouth would suddenly give way to the prettiest smile; the way she'd shift from cool, precise, and efficient to soft. Greg ran his hand across his eyes and tried to clear his head. Thinking of Chris wouldn't solve anything. Even while he was busy trying to save his team, in the back of his mind, he'd done nothing but think of her. He dreamed of her and imagined all the angry things he still wanted to say to her. Then he would want to take them all back again, wanting her back again, no matter what he had said or what she had done. Then he would remember it was the principle of the thing. Chris hadn't just cheated him, she'd practically killed off his team — his dream. Remembering that, Greg would get hurt and angry again.

Chris had phoned him twice. He had heard her voice on the answering machine, and he had pretended not to be home.

Now he jumped up from the couch and jammed his hands in the pockets of his light baggy slacks. He slipped his bare feet into his loafers and wandered over to the partially opened French doors. The damp, cool air felt refreshing. He took a couple of deep breaths. His chest felt tight. He had a pounding sensation in the back of his head and a knot right behind his eyes, as if he'd been sailing too long on the Bay without a hat. He felt like he'd had too much wind and sun, but he knew it was really too little Chris.

He leaned against the door frame and ran his finger absently up and down the slick, flippy leaf of a potted plant. Outside, below the terrace that extended out from the back of his house, the lights of Rose Hill blinked sadly in the rain.

The doorbell rang. At first Greg didn't react. The sound seemed to come from far away. It rang again, more insistent. Greg roused himself. "Coming!" he hollered, his voice a husky shout.

"Chris!"

She stood in the doorway and forced her eyes to stay on Greg's, though she shifted nervously from foot to foot, as if not quite sure she had made the right decision coming here. Chris hadn't seen him once around school for two days now. She had looked for him all over yesterday, and today she had waited by his locker. She seemed to run into every single one of Kennedy's two thousand students except for Greg. Chris was so happy to see him. He looked so wonderful standing there. Then she frowned. She realized he actually looked terrible. The color had faded from his usually ruddy cheeks. His eyes looked puffy and tired as if he hadn't slept, and his usually neat hair was sticking up at odd angles, almost in spikes. He looked like some crazy amalgam of preppy/punk.

"Uh, can I come in?" she finally asked, looking over Greg's shoulder. She hesitated at the door, afraid he would say no. He didn't say anything. He just stood there. Chris struggled to be brave and walk in. She looked back at Greg. He didn't look angry, but he didn't look inviting, either.

Finally he stepped aside.

As Chris passed into the imposing front hall, she brushed his arm. At her touch, his whole body tensed. She stifled the impulse to turn around and run out and give up this whole crazy notion that she could fix whatever was wrong between them. For Phoebe, love made anything work. But for people like Greg and Chris, maybe the rules were different.

"Are you alone?" she asked, even though on the way down the front walk she had noticed the garage door was open. His parents' Mercedes was gone. She wondered how long Greg would give her the silent treatment. She wondered if when he finally talked, he'd repeat the same kind of horrible things he'd said to her Monday in the auditorium.

Chris tossed her hair out of her face. It hung down loosely and was a little limp from the rain. She knew Greg liked it down more than braided, so she had worn it like this. She cleared her throat and pointed to the family room. "Can we talk?" She didn't wait for him to answer. She pushed open the door and stepped down into the spacious wood-paneled room. She waited for Greg to follow her. He did. He sat down on a bar stool and swiveled back and forth, keeping his eyes on her, waiting for her to begin.

She sat primly on the edge of the couch, her hands in her lap, clutching her bag tightly.

"I came here to say I made a mistake," Chris began with difficulty. "I went over the figures again. They were fair — I didn't try to cheat you. But I do think I bent over backward a bit so that no one could say I'd been partial, because you're. . . ." Chris faltered. "Because you're my — friend."

Greg was tempted to rush over to Chris and take her in his arms. He wanted to believe her.

170

He did believe her, but something kept him from letting her know that.

He stayed where he was and cleared his throat. At the sound, Chris looked up with a gleam of hope in her clear blue eyes.

Greg met her glance and said, "I owe you an apology, too. I flew off the handle Monday. I said things I shouldn't have. I didn't really mean a lot of what I said. I was so angry. . . ." Greg's voice was very controlled, but his eyes begged Chris to forgive him. "And about being fair or not, maybe it was a mistake, Chris. But how can I explain your mistake to my team? This is bigger than me and you. It's been bigger than both of us all along."

Greg stopped and braced himself to hear Chris's argument.

"I know. I thought about that myself. Then Phoebe pointed out I was back to keeping the letter of the law again and forgetting about the spirit of it. Crew did come out lowest in all of the standings — "

Greg frowned.

"But just by two points," Chris continued quickly. "That's not very much is it? It's not worth — it's just not worth all this."

For the first time in two days, Greg smiled. He raked his fingers through his hair. A moment later, the spikes popped up again. "So, apology accepted?"

"Apology accepted. Would you accept my help, too?" she added hesitantly.

Greg looked at her, puzzled.

"I tried to convince Principal Beeman to

change his decision. But he said my findings were correct." She got up a little and started toward him, still clutching her bag.

"I know," Greg admitted. "I talked to him myself."

"I'd like to help you in whatever way I can to raise money for crew. I've heard that you and Jonathan are planning some Save the Crew fund-raiser," Chris said.

Greg's smile widened. "Chris, when exactly are you going to schedule fund-raising sessions? As it is now, I practically have to set up appointments just to kiss you," he teased. He stopped swiveling his chair and looked at Chris. She had come halfway across the room toward him.

Greg cocked his head, trying to understand something, something he knew that Chris wanted, something that he wanted, too. He wanted to meet her halfway. What had been said on Monday was horrible, but he couldn't take back his words. So he crossed the rest of the room in three long steps and approached Chris. "I really love you," he whispered, wrapping his arms around her.

Her bag clattered to the floor. For a long time, neither of them moved. When Greg finally let her go, he bent down to pick up her purse. "What's this?" he said, holding a video tape in his hand.

Chris arched her eyebrows and pulled her sweater down over the top of her pants. "Uh, well it's sort of like our song," she said demurely. "I brought it along just in case we made up." She buffed her nails on her sweater sleeve and sat back down on the couch. "After all, if I'm going to be the first woman President, I'd better get used to planning ahead."

Greg pulled out the cassette and started to laugh. It was the movie they saw together on their very first date at the drive-in the summer before. "*Attack of the Killer Tomatoes*. I thought you hated this." He popped it into the VCR. Grabbing the remote control, he headed toward the couch, and flopped down, his head in Chris's lap.

"I might hate it," Chris said slowly, flicking out the lamp as Greg turned on the TV. "To tell you the truth," she said as she ran her finger very lightly down the side of Greg's neck, "I never saw enough of it to know exactly what I think."

"Do you think I'm going to let you now?" Greg said as the first frame flickered on the screen, and a housewife started screaming when a tomato bounced up from the sink and zapped her in the face.

Chapter
18

Eric slapped two more quarters down on the counter and folded his arms, waiting for the attendant to grab his prize from the shelf.

The Georgetown Cherry Blossom Street Festival was in full swing and the fairway was jammed with a rowdy Friday-night crowd. Eric was oblivious to the noise, the bustle, the stale, greasy french-fry-hot-dog stench in the air. Right after his meet, he had headed down here with Danny and Chip to work off some energy. His teammates had instantly found some girls and wandered off to the Ferris wheel. Eric had gratefully fallen behind. He had been in the mood for a noisy, crowded spot like this. Crowds were the perfect place to get lost in.

The beet-faced vendor was sweating as he shoved a giant stuffed Garfield cat into Eric's arms. He eyed the quarters on the counter and asked hopefully, "Haven't you had enough yet?"

Eric dumped the stuffed animal into the pile of prizes already at his feet and held out his hand. "Three more balls, please." The man reluctantly fished out the balls and stepped gloomily to the side of the booth. Eric juggled the first ball in his palm, then drew back his arm and tossed it. *SMACK*. Right on target, it toppled the pyramid of wooden milk bottles.

"All right!" Ted Mason's voice rang out. Eric looked over his shoulder, startled. Ted was there with Molly, Holly, and Bart. Spotting Molly, Eric stiffened a little. He looked behind her, but Katie wasn't with them. Eric ran his fingers distractedly through his hair. Of course she wasn't. Tomorrow was her big meet. She was probably home in bed right now.

"So this is how you fine-tune your pitches?" Bart nodded approvingly as he spotted the pile of prizes. By now, Eric had gathered a small crowd of onlookers. He had played ball-toss six times now — three dollars worth of quarters. He had already won twenty-five dollars worth of prizes.

Eric had two balls left. He heaved his arm back again and knocked the next pyramid to the ground. The vendor groaned. Eric didn't pay any attention. He threw his last pitch. This time he missed. The booth attendant beamed and turned to Ted.

"Hey, is this guy your friend? Get him out of here, huh? He's not so good for business."

Ted chuckled. "Grab your loot, Eric, and let's talk business. I think you are just the pitcher the Cardinals are looking for."

"Even if I sometimes throw a game?" Eric said.

"Are you still harping on that, Shriver?" Molly punched him lightly in the arm, then looked into his eyes.

Eric colored slightly and turned away. It was obvious Molly knew about him and Katie. It figured. Girls talked a lot about these things. Knowing Molly knew embarrassed him.

Ted expertly manipulated Eric through the throng. Eric looked around and noticed Molly, Holly, and Bart were nowhere in sight.

"Hey, where did everybody go?" Eric said. He dug at the pavement with the tip of his boot and avoided Ted's eye.

"I heard about you and Katie," Ted said, reaching in his pocket for some change, and getting two sodas from a concession. He tossed one can to Eric, then guided him behind the booths, where he sat down on the steps of a brownstone building.

Eric chose to stand. He leaned against the wrought-iron railing leading down from the steps and peeled back the metal top to his soda. "Everything Katie does these days is big news." His own bitterness surprised him.

Ted winced at Eric's comment. "Molly told me what happened. Do you want to talk about it?"

Eric turned his back to Ted and lifted his head to the sky and squinted, trying to see the stars. The downtown lights were too bright tonight. He couldn't even make out one star. With his eyes focused on the spot where the Big Dipper should have been, he said very quietly, "There's nothing to talk about. It's just not working." He shrugged.

"I really like her a lot. I've never dated a girl like Katie before — you know that."

Ted laughed. Eric had a reputation for liking the pretty sports groupies that tended to cluster around the campus gridiron heroes or team captains. He had the sort of looks that girls really liked.

"But instead of dating her, I feel like I'm running a race — *against* her all the time. A race I'm going to lose." Eric gave a self-disgusted snicker and dropped down to the bottom step. He propped his chin in his hands. "I guess you think I'm a bozo, huh?"

"No, not at all," Ted said.

He slugged down the rest of his Coke and worked a kink out of his powerful neck before continuing. "I met Molly down at the beach last summer. She was a lifeguard." Ted paused for a moment. "Well, I guess you know that!"

"Hey, man, I'm really sorry about the scene with Molly in lifesaving class. I — "

Ted cut him off with a thump on his back. "Come off it. I was just teasing. Anyway, the first time I tried to kiss her, she pulled one of those funny akido moves and, thump, there I was, flat on my back in the sand, hurting like I don't know what. I couldn't believe it! But you know what really hurt?"

Eric sat silently in the dark.

"My football-captain ego." Ted shook his hand in a gesture of pain and groaned at the memory. "But it didn't matter at all once the initial shock had worn off. I had met Molly and that was what mattered. I had to learn to deal with my feelings, and she had to deal with hers, too."

Ted's admission surprised Eric. "But do you feel jealous of her, Ted? I don't even want to go to the states tomorrow. I can't bear the thought of seeing her getting all the glory. And I hate feeling like this. It's so — " Eric jumped up and stuffed his hands in his jeans pocket.

"Small?" Ted suggested. "I feel like that sometimes. Molly can still flip me, you know." He laughed. "But being jealous is natural. You just have to deal with it."

"And then — " Eric went on haltingly, "I can't help feeling a girl like Katie just doesn't need me. She'll go on to win whether I'm there or not."

"You'd be surprised how much she needs you," Ted replied, standing up and stretching his arms high above his head, then bobbing over and touching his toes. "Speaking of needing people, here comes the rest of the crew. We're all heading to Annapolis early tomorrow on the bus." Ted paused and waited for Eric to change his mind.

"Even if I wanted to go, I can't go now." Eric explained about Garfield House, the swim sessions, and his dumb mistake about the dates.

"Hey, if you change your mind, call Molly. I bet she'd cover for you. Let her know if things look different in the morning."

"Maybe — maybe in the morning I'll feel differently," Eric said, sounding very doubtful as he followed Ted back into the fair. He hung a little behind the others, kicking at an empty soda can as he walked. Ted's story about Molly stuck with him. It made sense. They had worked out some of the same problems he had with Katie. But Katie wasn't Molly. And Ted, well, Ted was a different sort of guy. And anyway, Ted's Cardinals always won the division football title. Eric's team hadn't yet won a major meet. Eric didn't like himself for envying Katie, but he didn't know how to turn off his feelings: his jealous feelings or his feelings of love. He felt like there was some kind of war going on inside of him and he couldn't predict the outcome.

He looked around the festival booths, restlessly searching for some game to play or something to do. Eric needed something to take his mind off Katie, his talk with Ted, and the decision he sensed deep down inside he had already made.

Chapter
19

The turntable whirred. A blast of static cackled through the sound system of the Annapolis Heights Park Arena, followed by the scratchy introduction to a John Philip Sousa march.

Pale but determined, Katie Crawford turned to the group of five girls on the ramp leading from the dressing rooms, and attempted a smile. "Okay, troops, this is it. Let's give it our best!" After a moment they fell back in line again. Katie tugged down the back of her bright red leotard. With a firm set of her jaw, she marched into the arena, leading the Kennedy High team in the ceremonial opening parade of the Maryland State Gymnastics Tournament.

Katie felt the parade part of the meet was extremely hokey. Usually she would have had a hard time keeping a straight face at something like this. All these teenage kids marching around looking so solemn and serious. But today she looked pretty solemn, too. She didn't have the heart to smile. She wasn't even sure she had the heart to compete. Of course, she knew somehow she would because she had to. Wednesday night, something inside of her had snapped together, like pieces of a puzzle. Katie suddenly understood herself better. She knew the kind of person she was. She had to do her best. For herself and for her team. Loving Eric, or losing him, wouldn't change that. She'd get through this competition. In a few more hours, for her at least, the gymnastic season would be over and at last she could let go inside, let herself cry until there were no more tears. Then she would get up and begin again as if Eric had never happened.

As she rounded the far end of the arena she held her head high, keeping her eyes fixed on the back of the girl in front of her, a tall blonde from a Baltimore school whose picture had been on the cover of last month's *International Gymnast*, the competition's probable overall winner.

"Way to go Katie Crawford!" A shout rang out from the bleachers. Katie stole a peek out of the corner of her eye. At first she couldn't make out the faces. Then she saw Sasha with her boyfriend Rob. Jeremy Stone waved a camera in her direction. She saw Fiona, Dee, and then Chris and Greg. Katie started to smile. They were back together again. Holly and Bart, Karen and Brian, Elise and Ben must be there, too. She took another quick look. "Ted," she cried over the Sousa finale, forgetting all about Coach Muldoon's warnings about being dignified. Next to Ted should be

Molly. Katie peered intently, searching the stands. The whole gang cheered. Then Katie rounded the next bend in the arena. Halfway down the exit ramp, she wondered how she had missed Molly and her usual loud, raucous cheers.

Katie was the next girl up. This was her last event of the season. The rest of the team had finished their round and the scores had been pretty sensational. Katie's tumbling routine was the last event of the Kennedy team. She stood on the sidelines, stretching her legs, and eagle-eyeing a girl from Carrolton. The girl went into a double flip and flubbed her landing. Katie flinched, but the audience cheered anyway. As the girl bowed, first to the right side of the arena, then the left, Katie stepped onto the edge of the mat. She glanced up at the grandstand to the right of the scoreboard, looking toward her friends. She gasped. Eric was there, waving and yelling in her direction, flashing her a thumbs-up sign.

Then the announcer's voice called her name. Katie willed herself to tune Eric out. Miraculously, her heart stopped racing, her mind emptied of everything but a picture of her routine from start to finish. The warning light went on, the music started and Katie's body flew into motion. She leaped, twisted, soared through the air, handspringing her way across the mat, then sticking her ending like glue.

When the crowd began to cheer and clap, she flashed a triumphant smile and bowed, one time to each direction in the arena, saving the right side until last. When she came up, she sought

Eric's eyes. She bounced joyously out of the spotlight, yanked on her sweats, then bounded back again to see her scores flash up on the board. They were terrific, and she jumped up and down with her hand over her mouth, trying not to scream. She bowed once more, then looked up again for Eric. He was gone from the stands. When she skipped down the exit ramp, she landed straight in his arms.

Later on, she knew he must have said something. She knew he did, but she had no idea what, except her name — that wild, beautiful way he had of saying it. He picked her up and spun her around so fast she thought she would fly out of his arms back out into the arena like some kind of huge, crazy bird.

When he finally set her down, he said, "Let's go somewhere else. Somewhere we can be alone. I want to talk to you." His voice sounded urgent, full of feeling, and very proud. He shot a quick glance around the arena, his face clouding with uncertainty. He rumpled his wavy hair through his fingers and glanced back at the judges stand. "Can we? I mean, is it okay for you to leave? Is there an announcement, a ceremony?"

Katie had no idea if it was okay but she knew she didn't really care just then. For an answer, she took his hand and led the way behind the dressing rooms to the vast space of the loading docks and storage areas. Right there, between a bright red dumpster and some kind of forklift, she wrapped her arms around his neck and kissed him. A round of cheers rumbled toward them out of the arena, and Katie felt absurdly happy. She snuggled more deeply into Eric's arms and buried her nose in the side of his neck.

She had done extremely well today. She hadn't won, but she had done her best, and Eric had seen her. Each time he looked at her now, she shivered. He looked so happy, so proud. The look from the other day, the resentment, was gone. She felt the slightest twinge of disappointment knowing that the season was over. But mostly, she felt terrific. It was the end of April, the middle of spring, and a new beginning for her and Eric. She lazily wound the fingers of one hand through his hair and traced his profile with the other.

"K.C.?"

She looked into his eyes. Eric's face was about an inch from hers. He was leaning on his elbows looking down at her. She pulled him even closer, wanting to kiss him.

Eric shook his head and gently pushed her away. He sat up and circled his knees with his arms. "We have to talk," he said.

"No we don't. Not really."

Eric reached over and cupped her cheek in his palm. "We do, really." He paused and moistened his lips. "I'm not great with words," he began, "but I guess 'I'm sorry' will do for starters. I've been very mixed up about us. I've never been in love before, let alone with a girl who's a real champ. Each of your wins felt like a loss for me, and I resented you for that."

Katie inhaled sharply. She reached for his hand and squeezed it, but she didn't interrupt. She could see how hard it was for him to say all this. She didn't need to hear it, but somehow it was important for Eric to get it out in the open the way she had with Molly the other night.

"I kind of looked at you as a rival." Eric shook his head as if he could hardly believe what he was saying.

Katie couldn't let him go on. "Eric, I felt like that, too. I was so afraid you'd win the states at Virginia Prep, and I'd lose in Potomac. I got so worked up over that thought, I went out and scored a perfect ten," she confessed. She thought for a moment by telling him she risked losing him. But not telling him would be wrong.

Eric stared at her dumbfounded. "You mean that?"

Katie gave an embarrassed laugh. "I mean it. And believe me, it didn't make me feel very good. And then I realized that you felt the same way about me." Suddenly Molly's words Wednesday night came back to her. She tried to remember them exactly. She wanted to share them with Eric. She wanted him to understand. "There's no reason we can't be rivals and love each other, too." She held her breath waiting for his response.

The dimple in his right cheek deepened. "You're right! There's no reason at all!" he cried out.

"But I want to tell you from here on in — " Eric put his hand on Katie's shoulders and made her face him squarely. "I'm going to go out there and try to win. I know you're going to do the same. But win or lose, you matter more to me than all the prizes, trophies, and medals in the whole world."

Katie laughed. Her eyebrows arched up. She

sat back on her heels with a wicked glint lighting up her brown eyes. "You mean I matter more to you than bringing your team to the states next year — "

Eric nodded.

"Than pitching Kennedy High to victory this spring?"

Eric nodded again.

Katie squinted and leaned very close to Eric. "You liar!" she accused and started laughing as she pummeled him lightly with her fists.

Eric laughed, too, loud and full and hearty, the joyous sound echoing against the metal rafters. He fended off her blows and captured her by the wrists. They sank down together onto a soft heap of old burlap sacks piled in a corner of the loading zone. The laughter died on Eric's lips, and he gazed at her with eyes full of love.

"Okay, okay. But would you believe me if I said at the moment all I want to win is your heart?"

Katie's voice caught in her throat. "In that event, you've already clinched the gold," she whispered, just before his lips met hers.

Coming Soon...
Couples #21
TEACHER'S PET

"Well, Susan," her teacher said, scrutinizing her through round, gold-rimmed glasses. "You certainly didn't do well on your test."

Susan cleared her throat to prepare to defend herself. "I should have studied harder," she admitted weakly.

"Did you study at all?"

"A couple of hours."

"That should have been enough to pass the test." Miss Taylor tapped her pen on the desk briskly. "Didn't you understand the problems, Susan?"

"Yes . . . well, no. I guess not. I mean I must not have, or I would have gotten a better grade." Susan studied the stitching around the toes of her loafers, her cheeks pink with unhappiness and embarrassment.

"Pulling up this grade is going to take some

work. Hmmm." Miss Taylor pressed her lips together as she thought. "I've got it," she said, her face brightening. "Colin Edwards."

"Who?"

"Colin is a junior and one of my best students. He has a lot of tutoring experience — he does it after school for extra credit. Would you be interested in working with him?" Miss Taylor asked. "He'll be here any minute now."

"Well. . . ." Susan stalled for an answer. She wasn't exactly thrilled at the prospect of spending afternoons going over algebra equations with a nerd.

Just then the door swung open and Susan turned her head, her silky ponytail swinging. She stopped herself just in time from gasping out loud. This guy couldn't possibly be her tutor. He was by far the cutest boy she'd ever seen.

Susan liked his whole manner — he looked confident enough to do anything he set his mind to. Self-assurance showed as much in his walk as in the way his eyes twinkled when he smiled, and he was smiling as he approached Miss Taylor's desk. As Susan watched him, she forgot to breathe a few times. Her heart was beating as if she'd just run five miles at a dead sprint.